Tidal Wave

the misadventures of Willie Plummet

PAUL BUCHANAN
& ROD RANDALL

CPH
SAINT LOUIS

The Misadventures of Willie Plummet

Invasion from Planet X
Submarine Sandwiched
Anything You Can Do I Can Do Better
Ballistic Bugs
Battle of the Bands
Gold Flakes for Breakfast
Tidal Wave
Shooting Stars
Hail to the Chump
The Monopoly
Heads I Win, Tails You Lose
Ask Willie
Stuck on You
Dog Days
Brain Freeze
Friend or Foe
Don't Rock the Float
Face the Music
Lock-In
A House Divided

Cover illustration by John Ward.
Back cover photo by Ira Lippke.
Cover and interior design by Karol Bergdolt.

Scripture quotations taken from the HOLY BIBLE, NEW INTERNATIONAL VERSION®. NIV®. Copyright © 1973, 1978, 1984 by International Bible Society. Used by permission of Zondervan Publishing House. All rights reserved.

Copyright © 1998 Rod Randall
Published by Concordia Publishing House
3558 S. Jefferson Avenue, St. Louis, MO 63118-3968
Manufactured in the United States of America

Library of Congress Cataloging-in-Publication Data

Buchanan, Paul, 1959-
   Tidal Wave / Paul Buchanan & Rod Randall.
     p. cm. — (The misadventures of Willie Plummet)
   Summary: Thirteen-year-old Willie Plummet, who has a talent for misadventure, calls on God's help when he inadvertently causes the local amusement park to be shut down as a safety hazard.
    ISBN 0-570-05086-3
    [1. Amusement parks—Fiction.   2. Christian life—Fiction.]
   I. Randall, Rod, 1962-   .   II. Title.   III. Series: Buchanan, Paul.
   PZ7.B87717Ti 1988
   [Fic]—dc21

                                             98-19609
                                              AC

3   4   5   6   7   8   9   10   11   12   10   09   08   07   06   05   04   03   02   01

For the youth of Harbor Trinity

Contents

1

Sky Dive

I stood at the top of Sky Dive, the highest slide in the water park. I pressed my forearms against my stomach and tried not to shiver. Water trickled past my feet. The giant black tube beneath me swallowed each drop, as if nothing could quench its thirst.

"Willie Plummet," I mumbled, in a feeble attempt to reassure myself, "you're a dolphin, a water animal. This slide is your destiny."

Sky Dive was the nerve-shattering attraction of Slick Slides Water Park, capable of scaring even a tough-as-nails adventurer like myself. Kids waited for hours to brave the black tube that dropped and twisted like a giant corkscrew. But not today. There wasn't a kid in sight.

I couldn't figure it out. Kids stood in line at other water slides, why not this one? Maybe this year's crop of cream puffs didn't have the guts for it. Then again, maybe it didn't have anything to do with the kids.

Maybe something was wrong with the slide. That made more sense, even though there was no out-of-order sign posted.

I stared down the dark tube. A dull rumbling echoed from its depths, like the noise that comes from my older brother Orville's stomach when he skips a meal. A cool breeze gave me goose bumps. Common sense said turn around and go back. But in 13 years of living, no one had ever used the words "common" or "sense" to describe me.

I chanced a look down the steps that had brought me here. Good thing I did. Leonard "the Crusher" Grubb, the thug of Glenfield Middle School, paused at the entrance to Sky Dive. If I wimped out now, Crusher would have me for lunch. He'd blab to all my friends. I'd be "Plummet the Pansy" to everyone. I'd have to transfer to another school—or planet.

I breathed, "Help me, God," and took a step forward. Sometimes a good-looking guy's got to do what a good-looking, red-headed, brave, intelligent guy's got to do. The black throat of Sky Dive gargled with anticipation.

"Banzai!" I sprang forward, dove into the tube, and landed hard on my belly. "Look out below!"

As I plunged downward, water splashed in my face. I tried to deflect the spray with my hands, but that only made it worse. I slid deeper. The tube flung me from side to side.

"Yes!" I hollered. I was totally out of control and loving it. "This slide rules, and I have it all to myself."

Then something knocked my ribs.

"Ouch!" I blurted out. *Thump*! It did it again. *Thump*! And again. Sky Dive was defective. The seams where the black tubes connected had shifted just enough to create a ridge.

I rolled onto my back, but that didn't help. And to make matters worse, at each crooked seam, water dripped from the tubes, leaving less for me to slide on.

I plunged faster and faster, scraping and thumping as if in a giant cheese grater. No wonder Sky Dive was deserted. My skin heated from the friction against the pipes. I slid farther. My skin got hotter.

"Yeow!" I wailed as I dropped like molten lead. *Scrape, thump, burn.*

I descended with the force of a meteor. Then my face collided with a nest of long strands of plastic tape. What now? I tried to untangle myself. It felt like being tied with a thousand yards of ribbon. But this ride was no gift. The sides of the tube rubbed my skin raw. The misaligned seams knocked me senseless. *Scrape, thump, burn.*

I couldn't take much more. Thankfully, I didn't have to. *Swoosh*!

I launched into open air and splashed into the receiving pool. Kicking to the surface, I gasped for air. A web of soggy yellow tape clung to my skin. I yanked and twisted to free myself as I swam to the side. A lifeguard met me there, followed closely by Sam, whose blonde hair looked perfect, like she was at church instead of a water park.

Sam was one of my best friends and would normally have joined me for the ride down the water slide. But today all she could think about was setting up fake interviews so she could practice for an internship she wanted with a local news station. The management had developed a program to involve junior high kids in covering student activities.

"What do you think you're up to?" the lifeguard fumed. He was about six-foot, four-inches tall with Hollywood hair and a perfect tan.

"That's a good question, Willie," Sam added before I could answer, apparently more impressed with the lifeguard than with me. "What *are* you up to?" She held a tube of sunscreen in front of my face like a microphone.

"Four hundred degrees," I gasped between breaths. "That ride cooked me like a sausage."

Sam moved the tube of sunscreen to the lifeguard. "Any comments?"

"That's what he gets for removing the tape," the lifeguard said. "Sky Dive is closed. Can't he read?" He unwound the yellow tape from my shoulders and held it up. The words CAUTION! KEEP OUT! were written in big black letters along the tape.

"Any indication as to why he did it?" Sam asked, still holding the sunscreen/microphone in front of the lifeguard.

The lifeguard shook his head in frustration. "I guess he's looking for a reason to get kicked out!"

"I never saw the tape," I said in my defense.

"How could you miss it? It was across the mouth of Sky Dive. We put it there to make sure no one took the slide. It's not safe."

"Tell me something I don't know."

Sam moved the sunscreen/microphone back and forth to keep up with our conversation. She followed everything we said with a fascinated, intense expression. It was unreal.

Then Felix ran up and stood on the edge of the pool. Unlike Sam, his hair was wet. Drops of water shimmered on his glasses and brown skin. One look at me and he shook his head in disbelief. "Willie, look at yourself! Your skin is all red and puffy."

"Not only that," Sam added, speaking into the tube of sunscreen, "it's steaming. Stand back, Felix. Willie's about to spontaneously combust."

"If I do, blame Sky Dive," I growled.

"You can't blame Sky Dive for the chicken pox," Felix went on. "And now you've contaminated the whole park." When a case of chicken pox had hit Glenfield the week before, Felix had turned paranoid. Somehow he had missed getting them when he was younger.

"Knock it off. I had the chicken pox when I was 5." I explained what happened in the black tube, certain Felix would come to my defense.

"Way to go, Willie," Felix said. "My dad got us free passes and you show your gratitude by breaking the rules."

The lifeguard glared with conviction.

"He makes a good point," Sam put in, returning the tube to my face. "Your remarks?"

I was about to renew my protest when a loud wailing erupted from Sky Dive. We turned to look just as a giant splash washed over us.

"Sounds like someone else got the torture treatment," I said, sort of glad I wasn't the only one to suffer in Sky Dive—at least until I saw who it was.

Leonard Grubb rose to the surface of the pool, coughing and breathing fire. Steam rose from the water around his skin.

I joined Sam and Felix on the outside of the pool as the lifeguard helped Crusher.

"What do you think he's telling the Grubbster?" I wondered out loud.

"I don't know, but he keeps pointing to the caution tape, then you, Willie," Sam replied.

"That can't be good," I concluded. I was right.

"Plummet!" Crusher shouted. "You're dead meat!"

"That's funny," Sam noted. "Even Crusher wants to turn you into a sausage."

"What now?" Felix asked.

"One word," I said, kicking it into high gear. "Run!"

I took off through the water park at a full sprint. Sam and Felix followed. It's not that they had anything to fear, but we were such good friends, we tended to stick together no matter what. And for three eighth-graders, we made quite a team. Felix's genius IQ would rival a college professor's. Sam dominated in almost any sport. And my specialty was inventions. Thanks to the lab in the storeroom of Plummet's Hobbies, my dad's shop, I could whip up an invention for just about any adventure.

Right now, I wished I had the time to whip up a pair of rocket-powered skates.

"You're mine, Plummet!" Crusher growled, closing in.

We sprinted through the kiddy fountain where children floated on tubes. Crusher thundered behind us like a water buffalo. As the bully of Glenfield Middle School, his specialty was dishing out pain, not taking it.

"Quick! Around here!" I said. We ran behind the massive aquarium near the entrance to the park. It featured Happy the Hammerhead, a motorized shark that everyone made fun of. Last year, Crusher had carved his initials in Happy's head. From the aquarium we cut into the courtyard of the administrative building.

"Now what?" Felix asked.

"This way," I said. An exterior flight of stairs led to the second floor. At the top, we crammed against the door, hoping Crusher wouldn't see us.

He did. The building shook as he marched up the stairs.

Instinctively, I turned the knob. The door opened and the three of us fell into the room. Looking up, I was so shocked by what I saw, my problem with Crusher no longer mattered.

So Long, Slick Slides

Mr. Patterson, Felix's dad, sat at a long table, glaring at us over his glasses. Several men and women sat on either side of him. Everyone wore business suits. They greeted us with frowns. At the head of the table sat an elderly man with white hair. He folded his hands, his fingers ringed with gold, and glared at us in judgment.

"Nice entrance, kids," Mr. Patterson said. "I see you're in top form today."

"Goodness gracious!" a woman exclaimed. "What's wrong with the red-headed boy?"

A man with a pencil behind his ear leaned over the table. "It's chicken pox! Stay away from him. He's as contagious as the day is long."

A few people leaned backward and covered their faces. The rest wagged their heads in sympathy.

"I wish it were chicken pox," I said, climbing to my feet. "They wouldn't be *this* painful."

No one seemed convinced that I didn't have chicken pox, so, just for fun, I moved closer to the table. Everyone squirmed.

"That's close enough, young man," the man with the gold rings ordered. "Some of us never had chicken pox as children. And we certainly don't want them now!" He produced a cane from under the table.

Suddenly, joking around no longer seemed wise, so I explained what had happened on Sky Dive. I emphasized the terrible condition of the joints in the tubes and how much they hurt. I even directed the group's attention to Crusher Grubb, who was standing outside the open door. One look from the executives and he bolted.

That's when Felix's dad spoke up. "You've all met my son, Felix. But allow me to introduce his two best friends, Samantha Stewart and Willie Plummet."

I waited for the usual "Good to meet you" or "How do you do?" But that's not what we got.

"I've heard enough!" the man with the gold rings on his fingers announced.

The room grew silent as everyone waited for his next remark. I glanced at Sam, fearful she'd whip out her makeshift microphone and hold it to his wrinkled, quivering lips. But she held her arms pressed to her sides, looking as nervous as I felt.

"If Mr. Plummet isn't safe at Slick Slides, nobody's safe," the elderly man stated. He rapped his cane on the long table. "Closing one slide won't cut it. After today, I'm shutting down Slick Slides for good!"

I stared at Felix in awe, too stunned to speak.

"Way to go, Willie," Sam muttered under her breath.

"At least now you have something to report," I shrugged, trying to deflect her wrath. Like the rest of the students at Glenfield Middle School, Sam came here as often as she could. She loved the place. And so did Crusher. He already was mad at me. I couldn't imagine how he would handle this news. I really would have to leave the planet.

"Ladies and gentlemen," the elderly man continued, "I'll leave it to you to notify your departments. As of closing time today, Slick Slides is no longer open for business. Meeting adjourned."

With that, papers were shuffled, pens returned to pockets, and notebooks closed. But not a word was spoken. Everyone quickly filed from the room, leaving Felix, Sam, and me huddled together in the center of the room, too stunned to know what to say.

Other than us, Felix's dad was the only one to remain behind. Rather than look at us, though, he stared out the window.

"Dad, are you okay?" Felix asked.

"I'm fine, son," Mr. Patterson replied, his voice soft. "I'm trying to come to grips with what just happened here. I didn't tell you kids this before, but I came today in hopes of getting a contract for my engineering firm."

"Oh, no," I groaned. My head dropped. No Slick Slides meant no more work for the current employees, let alone for people trying to get *new* contracts. "I'm sorry, Mr. Patterson. I didn't mean to mess things up for you."

"I know, Willie," he said softly. "You don't need to blame yourself."

"Yeah, leave that to me," Felix snapped, elbowing me in the ribs.

"And me," Sam added, tweaking my ear.

Mr. Patterson stepped between us. "Take it easy, kids. Things will work out all right. Sometimes life takes unexpected turns. So often it comes down to timing. And in this case, Willie's was ..."

"Horrible," I said.

"Disastrous," Sam added.

"Catastrophic," Felix announced.

I looked at Mr. Patterson, certain his word would be the worst. But he just winked at me and smiled.

"Perfect," he said, beaming from ear to ear. "Absolutely perfect."

"Huh?" I choked.

"We got the account," Mr. Patterson said. "We proposed that Slick Slides shut down for two months so our firm could renovate the entire place. The board of directors accepted our proposal just before you fell into the room. Your story about Sky Dive was icing on the cake."

"This is headline news," Sam announced. She fumbled for her tube of sunscreen as if it were a real microphone. "Covering this story is sure to get me that internship."

"Dad, what kind of renovations are we talking about?" Felix asked.

Mr. Patterson extended his palm toward the outside door. "If you're up for a tour, I'd be happy to show you. But brace yourselves—our plans are big."

"How big?" I asked.

"As big as a tidal wave," he announced. "Come see for yourselves."

We followed Felix's dad down the stairs and into the water park. He pointed out one planned project after another. "That small slide there will be torn down to make way for Big Niagara, a combination water slide and waterfall."

"How will that work?" Sam asked, resuming her sunscreen/microphone technique.

"You'll slide through a wide chute of several small drops, followed by a massive waterfall into a deep pool," Mr. Patterson explained.

"That sounds awesome!" I exclaimed.

"Yeah," Sam acknowledged. "I can't wait to try that one."

Mr. Patterson led us to an open space not far from the future site of Big Niagara. "You'll love the name of what's going in here: Flash Flood. It will feature the heaviest and fastest water flow of any water slide in North America. Sitting on an inner tube, you'll tumble through rapids, vertical turns, narrow chasms, and anything else we can think of to throw at you."

"I can't wait," I said. After hearing about several other new attractions, we found ourselves at the back of the park.

"Is that it?" Sam asked.

Mr. Patterson shook his head. "This area will feature Loop-to-Loop, the first water slide featuring not one but two complete loops, just like those you've seen on roller coasters."

"No way," I protested, convinced it was too good to be true.

"I know it sounds impossible," Felix's dad said with a laugh. "But it works on paper. The key is a high-speed free fall at the start."

I was too stunned to speak. The more I heard about the rides, the more I wanted to be part of the remodeling process.

"Where does Loop-to-Loop finish?" Felix wanted to know.

"I could tell you, but I'd rather show you." Mr. Patterson led us through the service door at the back of the park. From there we climbed a flight of stairs to a platform on the back of one of the water slides. "That's where," he said, pointing.

Sam, Felix, and I exchanged glances. Mr. Patterson pointed to a dirt field on the outside of the water park.

"Dad, that field is not even *in* the water park," Felix pointed out.

"Maybe not. But Slick Slides already owns the land. When we get done, that will be Pipeline Lagoon, the main attraction of the remodeled and renamed water park."

"Renamed?" Felix asked. "What's wrong with the name?"

"Are you kidding?" I cut in. "*Slick Slides* sounds like something you make in your backyard with an old swing set and sheets of wax paper."

"What will the new name be?" Sam asked, pushing the tube/mike in Mr. Patterson's face.

"*Tidal Wave*—home of the world's largest wave machine. It will be installed in Pipeline Lagoon and be capable of churning out giant waves with perfect curls." Mr. Patterson turned to face us. "So what do you think? Are you impressed?"

We all nodded and spoke at once.

"This rules," I said.

"Impressive and then some," Felix stated.

"I can't wait to report this to the TV station," Sam blurted out.

"Mr. Patterson," I said, "I want you to know that you can count on my help. I'll be here every day after school and all day on Saturday. No nails will be hammered or boards cut without me smack dab in the middle of it, doing my share."

"W-W-What?" Mr. Patterson choked. "Actually, there's no need for that, Willie. But thanks for the generous offer."

"It's my privilege," I continued.

Mr. Patterson started to speak but couldn't, obviously overcome with gratitude. I've had that effect on people before.

"Let the board of directors know I'll be here every step of the way," I added.

"That's v-v-very kind, but really, it's not necessary." Mr. Patterson flashed a quick nervous smile. "I'm sure you have other important responsibilities to keep you busy."

"Not really. Besides, I'd rather be here in the thick of things. Maybe they'll need me to help drive a tractor or bulldozer."

"A b-b-bulldozer?" Mr. Patterson winced, like he had just sunk his teeth into a lemon.

"Sure," I reasoned. "How hard could it be?"

"Well ... um ... I'm no expert, but I'm sure it takes some training," Mr. Patterson said.

"Training, schmaining. I'm your go-to guy on this project," I announced.

Mr. Patterson reached for something to lean on, evidently blown away by my generosity. "Actually, I'd prefer to involve you *after* the rides have been completed. You can test them first and give a report on how you like them."

Felix laughed. "You mean like a guinea pig?"

Mr. Patterson quickly elbowed his son. "Not at all. I prefer the title *test engineer*."

"Me too," I agreed with a confidant nod. "That sounds cool."

"Until then, don't feel obligated to come around," Mr. Patterson told me. "I'll let you know when we need you."

"What about me, Mr. Patterson?" Sam asked.

"You're welcome anytime. The more publicity the TV station brings us, the better. Our contract calls for the water park to re-open in two months. We'd love to have a news crew here for the festivities."

"What about me, Dad? How can I get involved?" Felix asked.

"Any number of ways, especially with your knack for problem solving. Mainly, I'd like you to provide a kid's-eye-view of the renovations. Can I count on you?"

Felix grinned. "You bet."

Mr. Patterson turned to leave with Felix on one side and Sam on the other. He rested an arm across each of their shoulders.

I lagged behind, still a little frustrated about my job. Trying out the new rides sounded great, but what would I do until then? Was I really unwelcome at the park? Mr. Patterson didn't really mean that, did he? Did he?

③ A Pro-Am Surf Contest

He did.

Every time I tried to join Felix at the water park, he had some lame reason why it wasn't a good day for me to come around. In the last two weeks, I hadn't been there once. Sam had been there several times. Instead of coming home from school and hanging out with my two best friends, I sat around, bored and lonely. Sometimes I watched TV, but that didn't help. I was so depressed, even the Three Stooges couldn't cheer me up.

"There's got to be something I can do at the water park," I mumbled to myself. Then it hit me. I could pray. If anyone could get me out of the doldrums, the Lord could. With my eyes closed, I asked for God's help. I asked Him to get me involved somehow in the remodeling of Tidal Wave.

When I finished praying, I opened my eyes. No bright light or angel from heaven greeted me. But I definitely felt better.

After a few more minutes of the Three Stooges, I decided to check my options on other stations. Picking up the remote, I skipped from channel to channel. I finally changed it to ESPN and decided to wait out the commercials in hopes that a decent program might be on.

In the meantime, I tried to call Sam. Maybe she had left the news station early and would want to hang out.

"Hello?" Sam's mom said, picking up the phone.

"Hi, Mrs. Stewart. Is Sam there?" I asked.

"No, and I don't expect her for a while. She called from the station to say she'd be late," Mrs. Stewart answered.

"Why? Have they asked her to broadcast the five o'clock news?" I said with a chuckle.

"Wouldn't that be nice. Unfortunately, things seem to be going in the opposite direction," Mrs. Stewart said. "Just so you know, the TV station hasn't been very impressed with her coverage of the water park renovations. She's concerned that the opportunity to broadcast student activities may go to someone else."

"How does she expect them to react when she uses a tube of sunscreen for a microphone?" I commented.

"Willie, you can be so funny sometimes," Mrs. Stewart said.

"Then why aren't you laughing?"

"This isn't one of those times."

Ouch! That hurt. I held the phone in silence.

"Actually, Sam has used a real microphone and brought along a real camera crew. But the station manager thought the stuff she brought in was boring," Mrs. Stewart explained. "At this point, all the station is willing to commit to is a short segment on the opening day ceremony. And even that may get bumped if a more interesting story comes along."

"Bummer," I said.

"In fact, the reason Sam is staying late is to gain back a little of the station manager's trust. She's hoping to score a few extra points."

"Well, I hope it works," I said. "Tell her I'll ..." Something I saw on TV forced me to stop mid-sentence.

"You'll what?" Mrs. Stewart asked.

I stared at the image as if hypnotized.

"Willie? Are you there? You'll what?" Mrs. Stewart repeated.

"Pray for her," I mumbled, still engrossed in the TV. With that I hung up and stared at the screen.

In front of me, a massive translucent blue image caught my attention. It was a wave but not just any wave. It was a giant blue breaker with a barrel hollow enough to drive a truck through. I watched in awe as

the curl peeled perfectly along, from one side of the
screen to the other.

Then the announcer broke in. "Good afternoon
and welcome to the Hawaii Surf Classic. Today you'll
see pros and amateurs alike riding one perfect wave
after another."

The scene cut to a surfer making a deep bottom
turn in the bowl of a wave. Then he stood back on his
board, gliding along the wave's face as the curl peeled
over his head. Another shot showed a surfer flying
from the wave's lip and wiping out. Still another had a
surfer dropping straight down the face of a giant
wave, then tumbling over the front of his board. Other
scenes showed pro surfers shooting out of tubes,
floating on white water, and turning so hard they
were practically sideways. And amazingly enough,
they rarely fell.

"That's it!" I said out loud. God already had
answered my prayer. Tidal Wave could hold a surf
contest on opening day. If they offered a big prize, pro
surfers would flock from around the world. Sam
could cover the biggest sports event to hit Glenfield
ever. And I could enter the amateur part of the contest. I already knew how to water-ski and skateboard.
I had even gone snowboarding a few times. How hard
could surfing be?

I decided to tell Sam right away. If she liked the
idea, the two of us could pitch it to Felix's dad. With
his support, the park directors would go for it.

Running outside, I got on my bike and rode to the TV station on the outskirts of Glenfield. After locking up the frame and wheels, I pushed through the front door to the lobby.

But that's as far as I got.

"Hold on there," the security guard said. His blue uniform looked a few sizes too small for his stout frame. He walked around the counter and stood between me and the studio door. "Where do you think you're going?"

"I have an important message for Sam Stewart, one of your future interns," I answered. "She's the one who uses a tube of sunscreen for a microphone."

The security guard didn't even crack a smile.

I offered a sheepish chuckle. "Not funny to you either, huh?"

Flipping through the pages on his clipboard, the security guard found what he was looking for. "Here she is, Samantha Stewart. Well, she's definitely in the studio, but I'm not sure you can visit her."

"I just need to tell her something real quick. It won't take long."

The security guard looked me over, then extended the clipboard. "Go ahead and sign in. You can find her through those doors. She's at the end of the hall in Studio A. But be quiet. They're ready to broadcast the five o'clock news."

"No problem, dude," I said, trying to sound like a surfer. I stepped quickly to the door while flashing the security guard a hang loose sign. If only I had noticed the sign.

Wham!

Pushing a door that reads *Pull* is as loud as it is painful. The bang rang out as if the lobby were an echo chamber. I tried to make light of it. "Glad I got that out of the way. From here on out, I'm a stealth messenger," I said.

I felt the security guard's glaring eyes on my neck even after the hall door closed behind me. Tiptoeing to Studio A, I quietly stepped inside. The room was the size of a small theater and packed with all kinds of equipment. Lights hung from the ceiling on steel girders. Cameras rested atop heavy stands with wheels. Microphones dangled over the desks where the newscasters sat. People moved in all directions. I guessed they were the technicians, producers, and directors that made it all happen.

Now all I had to do was find Sam. I stepped over cables and around props looking for her.

The news team moved into position on the set. The anchorwoman, Susan Hunter, sat down with a stack of papers in her hand. She wore a bright red coat and white blouse. Bill Decker, the anchorman, sat next to her. He was dressed just as sharply in a blue blazer and tie. His black hair, accented with a touch of gray on the sides, looked perfect. A makeup woman dabbed at Bill's nose, then moved over to Susan.

"Quiet on the set," a guy wearing headphones announced.

Not a problem, I thought. I couldn't find Sam and no one else seemed to know I was alive. Who *would* I talk to? The crew was so stressed over getting the news out, they didn't pay any attention to me.

I moved closer to the set and stood behind a guy sitting in a folding chair. He had a gray beard and wore a white ball cap. Looking down, I realized the chair said *Director*.

Watching everyone made me uptight, which made Sam's timing all the worse.

"Huh? What?" I said when she tapped me on the shoulder from behind.

"*Shhh*," the director hissed, holding his finger in front of his lips.

Sam quickly pulled me away from him.

Before I could tell her my idea, the guy with the headphones warned everyone again. "Quiet on the set. Five. Four. Three. Two. One. Rolling. And … action." He pointed at Susan Hunter.

"In our top story tonight," Susan said, staring at the camera with the red light, "congressional leaders seeking tax reform continue to blah, blah-blah …"

I stared at Sam, eager to give her my big news. I couldn't keep it in any longer. But she couldn't read my mind. She motioned for me to be quiet, then turned her attention to the broadcast.

As Susan Hunter droned on, I wondered how much more I could take. If I remembered correctly, the five o'clock news lasted for an hour. There was no way I could wait that long to speak. I wasn't even quiet that long in my sleep. Besides, I had told my parents I'd be right back. I tapped Sam on the shoulder, but she just shook her head.

What now? I fumed, looking around. Then I got an idea. I could write down my plans for a surf contest. With all the clipboards around, it shouldn't be hard to find an extra pen and paper—or so you would think. After searching the studio, I came up empty. Every clipboard in sight was in the clutches of a stressed-out technician.

Just as I was about to resign myself to a long wait, a better option caught my attention. There was a computer behind one of the cameras. Just as I spotted it, the guy sitting there stood up and exited through one of the side doors.

Yes! Talk about perfect timing. The guy obviously was done with the computer for now. I could type in a short explanation of my plan and make Sam take a look.

Working my way over to the computer, I noticed that the screen already was covered with words. Rather than read something I wasn't supposed to, I quickly hit *Enter* to start a new paragraph. After Sam read my message, I'd simply delete it. I'd leave the computer just as I had found it. No harm done.

Glancing from side to side, I sat down and pecked away at the keyboard as fast as I could.

Sam, kiss the boring news good-bye.
Tidal Wave will host a Pro-Am Surf Contest
for its opening day celebration. It will be
Glenfield's biggest sports event ever. You can
cover the event. And I, Willie Plummet, soon-
to-be surf legend, will dominate the competi-
tion and win!

I waved Sam over to take a look. As she arrived, something strange happened. Susan Hunter began to broadcast what I had written.

"Sam, kiss the boring news good-bye," Susan began.

Suddenly everyone shifted into panic mode. Papers shuffled on clipboards. Heads snapped in every direction.

"… Tidal Wave will host a Pro-Am Surf Contest," Susan Hunter continued.

"Willie," Sam hissed through gritted teeth, "you typed into the teleprompter. Whatever appears on the monitor also appears in front of the camera for Susan or Bill to read."

"Yikes!" I squealed. Reaching over, I moved the cursor to the start of my message and held down the *Delete* key.

"No!" the director hissed. He rushed over and stared at the screen. By then it was too late.

Susan Hunter announced my entire message before realizing what had happened—or how lost she was. To make things worse, I had deleted not only what I had typed, but some of the news script as well. In a moment of panic, Susan began to mix the real news with my message.

"Congressional surfers will gather for a pro-am tax contest," she explained, sweat beading on her powdered nose.

That's when Bill Decker took over. He had managed to locate the actual news script on the papers in front of him. But even he had a tough time getting back on track.

The veins in the director's neck strained so tightly that I thought they would pop. He grabbed my arm and held me tightly until he could cut to a commercial. Then he cut into me.

"That was totally irresponsible!" the director yelled, his face redder than Susan Hunter's suit coat. "I want you and Sam out of this studio. Wait for me in my office."

"But I was just—"

"I don't want to hear it!" he shouted.

Each time I tried to explain, the director got more upset.

"Quiet on the set," the guy with headphones announced.

"Move it!" the director growled. He threw his ball cap to the ground for emphasis.

Sam led me from the studio as the countdown began. "Five. Four. Three …"

We walked to the director's office. After closing the door, Sam picked up where he had left off. "That was your all-time greatest blunder, Willie."

"Don't you start," I said. "I came here to help you. A Pro-Am Surf Contest is big news."

"Yeah, for someone *else* to cover. After today, I'm fired for sure. Couldn't you just wait until the broadcast was over?"

"It was such a great idea—I couldn't keep it inside. How could I know Susan Hunter would read my message on the air? Although, that comment about congressional surfers was pretty funny. Good thing Decker took over or she would have drowned somewhere between the White House and Hawaii."

"What's funny about that? This is Susan's career we're talking about. Days like today could keep her from getting promotions," Sam said.

"Sorry," I said, getting defensive. "I didn't do it on purpose. I just wanted to give you my idea without waiting around for an hour."

"Then maybe you should learn a little patience or self-control," Sam huffed. She dropped her face into her hands.

"You're right," I said, having lost the will to argue. Seeing Sam so depressed brought someone else to mind. Felix's dad. Soon everyone in Glenfield and the surrounding towns would be talking about the surf contest. If the owners of Tidal Wave didn't like my idea, his job might be in jeopardy too.

After finding a phone book, I picked up the phone on the director's desk and dialed the number for Mr. Patterson's company. His secretary put me right through.

"Willie, what have you done?" Mr. Patterson asked, his voice exasperated.

"I take it you saw the news?" I asked.

"No, but I heard about it," Mr. Patterson replied.

"I'm sorry. I just wanted Sam to see my idea. I never—"

"I just got off the phone with the chairman of the board of the water park," Mr. Patterson cut in. "He saw the newscast. And you won't believe what he said."

"I don't want to know."

"Yes, you do. He loved the idea," Mr. Patterson said. "He wasn't thrilled about having it announced before he had approved it, but the concept of a world-class surf contest went over big. Really big. He thinks it will be great for publicity."

"That's awesome," I said. "Would you mind telling Sam's boss what you just told me?"

"Not at all. The more press involvement the better."

I breathed a big sigh of relief and thanked Mr. Patterson for being so understanding. After hanging up, I filled Sam in on what had happened.

Sam beamed. "Willie, this is too good to be true. Getting the scoop on a big news story is what reporting is all about. This should definitely change the director's attitude."

It did … to a point. The fact that the rest of the news went off without a hitch also helped. By the time he showed up at his office, he wasn't quite so irate.

"I'm still not happy with what happened," the director said from behind his desk. He had just gotten off the phone with Mr. Patterson. "But at least the story is true, and we got the scoop on it."

I grinned at Sam. She was right.

When I got home, I was just in time for dinner. As I sat down at the table, my parents wanted to hear all about what had happened.

"It sounds like you got off pretty easy," my dad said.

"That's because it was such a great idea," I explained. "Think about it. Everyone wins: Tidal Wave, the news station, and especially me."

"You?" Orville choked. As my older brother, Orville had trouble accepting my implied superiority. "You really think you can win that contest?"

"What makes you think I can't?"

"Maybe the fact that you've never tried surfing in your life," Orville said, laughing.

"You don't even own a surfboard," my sister, Amanda, reminded me. She was two years older than Orville, and she tended to be just as skeptical of my epic potential in life.

"I didn't say I could win it *today*. I've still got six weeks. And what's so hard about buying a surfboard?" I asked.

"In Glenfield?" Orville asked.

He had a point. There wasn't a surf shop in, or anywhere near, Glenfield. Mainly because there wasn't an ocean anywhere near Glenfield. But the town had grown every year as people moved here from other states. Maybe a newcomer would have a used board to sell. I explained my idea to everyone.

"It can't hurt to run an ad," Dad agreed. "You may come across a good used board."

"So what if he does?" Orville asked. "You need waves to surf. I don't think standing on a surfboard in your room will accomplish much."

"The wave machine should be done before opening day. I can practice at the park," I said.

"How much before?" Amanda asked. "A week? That's not enough time."

As much as I hated to admit it, Orville and Amanda were right. "So all I need is another way to practice until then. There's got to be something I can do." The table grew silent as everyone tried to come up with ideas.

"What about putting the surfboard in a hammock?" Amanda offered. My sister was known more for her beauty than for her brains, for obvious reasons.

Orville stopped chewing. "Do you think the surfboard needs its rest?" he asked.

"No, silly. Willie could stand on the board while we swayed the hammock. He could work on his balance that way."

"I'm game," Orville offered. "I'll have Willie spinning upside down before I'm through."

"Oh, that sounds like fun," I moaned.

"I've got an idea," Mom suggested. "You can surf the wakes at Lunker Lake. All you need is a boat to pull you."

"Or a Wave Ruler XT," Dad added.

Not long ago I had bought a Wave Ruler XT, which is a lot like a Jet Ski or a Waverunner. The money to buy it came from a honeybee attractor that Felix, Sam, and I had developed.

"That's it!" I shouted. "Orville can pull me on the Wave Ruler XT while I surf. I can practice getting up, balancing, turning, cutting. That's a perfect plan."

"Sounds fine to me," Orville said. "I'm always up for a ride on the Wave Ruler. You come up with a surfboard and my truck's at your service. I'll take you to the lake anytime."

That was all I needed to hear. After dinner I'd place an ad, then wait for the calls to flood my house.

That night when I went to bed, I turned to the Book of Psalms. When our youth pastor first challenged us to read a chapter of the Bible a night, it had seemed impossible. Now I found myself looking forward to it most nights.

I was reading Psalm 37 when a couple of verses jumped off the page at me. "Trust in the LORD and do good; … Delight yourself in the LORD and He will give you the desires of your heart." Wasn't that the truth. Who would have thought one little prayer could make

things work out so well at the news station and the
water park. But I had trusted God and He had come
through in a big way. The more I thought about it, the
more it made sense. If God could save me from sin, of
course I could trust Him to give me the desires of my
heart.

Felix and the Beanstalk

Did I say I would wait for a *flood* of calls? What a joke. After three days, I hadn't received one call. *Drought*, yes. *Flood*, no. Fortunately the ad would run for a week. There was still hope. *Trust in the Lord*, I told myself. And think *surf*.

In the meantime I decided to pay a visit to Tidal Wave. I had a few things to do. One, I could soak up the compliments for my world-class surf contest idea. And two, I could check on how the remodeling efforts were coming along. I was especially curious to get a look at the Pipeline Lagoon.

"You sure they'll let you in?" Sam asked, peddling her bike next to mine. She had planned to go anyway, so we had decided to ride over together.

"Yep. I checked with Felix's dad last night. Thanks to the pro-am, publicity for the park keeps rolling in. Now I'm welcome at the park anytime, just like you."

"Sounds like you're on everyone's good side," Sam said. "Well, almost everyone's."

"What do mean, *almost*?"

"It's nothing," she said, avoiding my glance. "I wouldn't want to spoil your day."

"Go ahead. I can take it," I said, bracing myself for the worst.

"I had a talk with Crusher Grubb about your news announcement. He wasn't impressed," Sam said.

"When is he?" I muttered. "What'd I do this time?"

"You won't believe it, but every summer he spends two weeks at his aunt's in California. She lives right by the beach," Sam explained.

"Don't tell me. He thinks he can surf better than I can," I said.

"Yeah. And since you can't surf at all, he's probably right," Sam replied. "Anyway, I'd avoid him until the contest if I were you. He's still mad about the Sky Dive incident. He thinks you removed the yellow warning tape on purpose. Watching you get your name on TV as a future surf champion didn't help any."

"So what? Crusher's not happy unless he's mad. Besides, what's he going to do to me?" I asked.

"Probably nothing, but he did mention that it would be hard for you to win a surf contest with two broken legs," Sam replied. "Other than that you don't have a thing to worry about."

"How nice," I muttered.

When we pulled up to Tidal Wave, we checked at the administration office for Felix and his dad.

"They're somewhere in the park," the reception-ist said between phone calls. She refused to look at us and sounded annoyed.

"That's some welcome," I said as we exited the building. "I practically put this place on the map, and she didn't even acknowledge me. Does the word *gratitude* mean anything to her?"

"Does the word *conceited* mean anything to you?" Sam retorted. "If anyone deserves credit, it's God for getting us both out of the mess you made."

"Maybe so, but a simple greeting would have been nice. Something like, 'Good afternoon, Mr. Plummet, sir. Can I get you anything while Mr. Patter-son is summoned?' "

"Willie, you're such a dreamer," Sam said, laughing.

Walking through the park, we realized that the receptionist wasn't the only one stressed out. Workers rushed in every direction, even more frantic than the news crew at the TV station. From one end of the park to the other, construction was in full swing. A crane lift-ed the water chutes and rocks into place for Big Nia-gara. Artists painted the mountain scenery that sur-rounded it. Some of the water slides, including Flash Flood and Loop-to-Loop, also were coming together. Even Sky Dive looked well on its way to completion.

"Now if only we can find Felix," I said. When a guy wearing a hard hat ran past, I got his attention. "Excuse me. I'm Willie Plummet."

He just stared at me, then said, "And?"

I cringed in humility. Strike two on the recognition angle. "Um, have you seen Felix?"

"Felix who? The cat?" the man replied. Everyone's a comedian.

"Mr. Patterson's son," Sam explained.

"Oh, him. I think he's at Beanstalk," the guy said, walking away. "He was checking the seams."

"Beanstalk?" I said with a laugh. "What kind of dumb name is that?"

"Don't judge a book by its cover, Willie," Sam told me.

She was right. When we found Beanstalk, it looked as high as the clouds. All the tubes were painted green. The stairs were shaped like leaves and climbed in a spiral along the tubes.

"Now I know how Jack felt," I said as we worked our way upward.

"Do you think that's Felix?" Sam asked. She pointed to a shadow in the tube not too far from the top.

"P-P-Probably," I gasped, reaching the top of another flight of leaves. "Man, the air is thin up here."

"Seems fine to me," Sam said.

Once we got to the top, I held tightly to the rail. It was by far the highest ride I'd ever been on.

"Felix! Are you in there?" Sam shouted. A muffled response rose through the tube.

"That must be him," I said, crouching to peer inside the green tunnel at the ride's starting point. "Let's go see what he's doing."

"No way," Sam protested. "What if we slip? We'll slide right into him."

"We won't slip. The water's not on," I observed. "Have you ever walked on a slide in tennis shoes? You don't slip. Besides, I'd rather be in there than out here in the open air." I directed my voice down the tube. "Felix, we're coming down!"

More muffled words echoed in response. They sounded more intense than the first.

"Sounds like he can hardly wait," I announced. "Sam, are you ready?"

"Willie, you're crazy," Sam said. "This isn't just a normal slide. It's made from probably the most slippery material on earth."

"If that were true, why would it require so much water?" I reasoned. "Come on." I squatted down and waddled like a duck into the tube.

Sam followed a few feet behind. The first few steps weren't a problem—or the ones after that. Then the slide got steep.

That's when we had a problem. Suddenly Beanstalk looked like the throat of a green dragon. I eased down, trying to keep my balance. My feet slipped out from under me as if I were on ice. *Swoosh!*

So much for balance.

Time to Trust

As I started to plunge, I reached for Sam, but I couldn't grab her hand in time. The last I saw of her, she was clutching the outside rim of the tube, shaking her head at me.

"Look out below!" I shouted. I followed with: "*Fore! Banzai. Hit the dirt!*" I hoped to give Felix a chance to get out of the way.

Too bad it was a slim chance. Spiraling down a steep turn, I caught a glimpse of Felix in front of me. His eyes swelled with fear.

That was just before we made contact. Full contact. *Wham!*

I plowed into Felix like a falling giant. From there we dropped with increasing speed.

"Yeow!" Felix wailed, feeling the friction heat his body.

For some reason, I no longer felt it. Then I realized why. Felix was under me, forming a human sled.

Talk about a dilemma. I felt guilty sliding down on Felix, but if I rolled off, I'd feel the burn. I decided to ride it out, seeing no need for both of us to get singed.

Too bad Felix had other plans. He shoved me off and rolled onto his stomach.

"Ouch!" we both wailed.

Our heads snapped back and forth as we plunged and slid. After what seemed like forever, we shot from the bottom of the tube into the shallow pool. We landed hard. But at least the pool wasn't empty. Cool water had never felt so good.

Felix glared at me with fire in his eyes. "Way to go, Willie. That's your second water slide accident in two trips to the park. What's your excuse this time?"

I just shrugged. We pulled ourselves out of the pool and rested on the concrete walkway.

"Go ahead," Felix persisted. "Let's hear the wise-crack."

"Fee, fie, foe, fum," I offered, hoping for a laugh.

Felix silently shook his head.

"Get it?" I went on. "Jack and the Beanstalk? Fee, fie, foe, fum."

"That's not funny," Felix said, his eyes still raging.

"Felix, you're stressed out," I told him. "Lighten up and have some fun."

We sat there until Sam came running up. She immediately extended her hairbrush to Felix as if it were a microphone. "Wow, that was some spill. Any indication of how it happened?"

"Knock it off, Sam. You know it was Willie's fault."

Sam moved the hairbrush to me. "Your response?"

"It was an accident," I said, shrugging it off. "And as the park's official test engineer, it's my opinion that Beanstalk passes the slippery standard."

Sam returned the mike to Felix. "Willie seems to think the slide is slippery."

"Duh. Why do you think they call it a slide?" Felix growled. "Now get that fake mike out of my face." He grabbed the hairbrush from Sam and tossed it over his shoulder.

Sam stared at Felix in shock, then sat down on the edge of the pool and joined us for a sulk.

For the next 10 minutes no one said a word. All the while, I felt more and more guilty. I finally offered Felix an apology. "Sorry, dude. I just stopped by to see how things were coming along."

"Not good," Felix quickly informed me.

"What do you mean?" I asked. "The seams on Beanstalk felt fine to me. And believe me, after that ride I took on Sky Dive, I know what misaligned joints feel like."

"Willie, it has nothing to do with Beanstalk," Felix said.

"Then what's the problem?" I asked, totally confused. "Thanks to my idea, Tidal Wave is the talk of

the town. Everyone's looking forward to the surf contest on opening day."

"*That's* the problem," Felix answered. "You can't
believe how much pressure everyone is under to get
the renovations completed on time—including my
dad. He's working around the clock. Not only that,
there's still a chance he'll get chicken pox."

"Is that still going around?" I asked.

"Definitely. Three of the park's best workers are
out on sick leave. That means more work for everyone else."

Suddenly, the attitude of the receptionist made
sense. Glancing up, I watched as people moved at a
frantic pace. Trucks sped past, hauling giant tubes for
new slides. A guy holding blueprints shouted orders
to the driver of a cement truck.

We followed Felix through the fence at the back
of the park. "There's the biggest stress producer of
them all," he explained, "Pipeline Lagoon."

Tractors and bulldozers broke through the hard
ground, filling one dump truck after another. The
lagoon wasn't very deep yet, but its shape was already
taking form. The area was huge, easily big enough to
handle waves for surfing.

"It looks like it's coming along fine," I offered
with a shrug.

Felix shook his head. "There's still so much to do.
The cement needs to be poured, followed by the sand
bottom. There's supposed to be a waterfall installed

on the side. And don't forget the wave machine. It hasn't even arrived yet. Everything requires a building permit from the city, which means more delays."

"Okay, okay," I said, starting to get depressed. "I believe you."

"There's no way everything's going to get done on time," Felix went on. "And thanks to your big surf contest idea, every TV station in the state is going to report it. My dad will look like a total failure."

"I can relate to that," Sam said. It was the first time she'd opened her mouth since Felix had tossed her brush away. "I'm a terrible sports reporter. I ask stupid questions with obvious answers. Even my own friends hate being interviewed by me."

"We don't hate it," I said. "We just can't stand it."

"Oh, that makes me feel *way* better," Sam replied.

"Okay, so maybe things seem pretty bad," I admitted. "But we can't give up. Look at me. The five o'clock news introduced me as a future surf champion. But do I know how to surf? No. Do I own a surfboard? No. Am I close to getting one? No. If anyone has a reason to give up, it's me."

"Then why don't you?" Sam asked. "You're in worse shape than we are … by far."

I swallowed hard. "It comes down to one word: trust. God didn't bring us this far to ruin our lives. He has always brought us through before. I'm sure He will this time too."

"It's not that I doubt He can do it," Felix admitted. "But it's going to take a miracle."

"That's for sure," Sam added.

"Then that's what we'll pray for," I said. "And we won't doubt. We'll trust God and delight in Him and He'll give us the desires of our hearts."

"Sounds like good advice to me," Sam said. "What verse is that, anyway?"

I told her about reading Psalm 37. She stood up, paused for a moment, obviously thinking, then left to find her hairbrush. Felix wandered off to look for his dad.

Standing alone, I closed my eyes and prayed. I know Jesus said we could move mountains by faith, but what about water? At first the surf contest had sounded like such a good idea. And now I had sounded off about trusting God. But if things didn't start going our way soon, we'd all be drowning in failure.

⑦
Couch Surfing

When my newspaper advertisement didn't produce a surfboard, my trust began to sink. Every night I prayed, certain that the Lord would provide. But the ad came and went and still nothing.

To make things worse, Crusher Grubb circled me like a shark. The Sky Dive incident had started things off, and the prediction about winning the contest had made things worse. He had promised to get even. I didn't take it too seriously, but just to play it safe and avoid unnecessary damage to my vital organs, I opted to vary my routes home from school.

Today's course took me along the east side of town, which turned out to be the best and worst way I could have picked.

"Hey, Plummet! What are you doing over here?" a harsh voice demanded.

I glanced around, certain it was Crusher. But I didn't see anyone. I knew the voice had come from inside a house. But which one?

Then it occurred to me—I wouldn't know Crusher's house if it fell on me. In choosing a different route home, had I actually stumbled into enemy territory? Rather than stick around to find out, I ran around the corner and hopped the nearest fence.

But what greeted me was even scarier than Crusher Grubb.

To my horror, I stared right into the jaws of a shark. That's right. A shark! It was suspended at eye level, just inches from my red head.

I wanted to shriek in terror. But I stopped myself just as Crusher thundered past on the other side of the gate.

Then I realized that the shark was stuffed, as in dead. It rested on top of a bamboo cabinet. Next to the shark, other items relating to the sea hung from the wall: a life preserver, a fishnet, a few old fishing poles. Two scuba tanks stood against the garage wall. An old-fashioned anchor sunk into the lawn. Then I spotted the best item of all—a surfboard. It was leaning against the dryer, just inside the garage.

When Crusher's voice faded in the distance, I stood up and tiptoed along the side of the house. At the back door, I knocked lightly and waited. A short while later a man in a red Hawaiian shirt appeared. He had thinning blond hair and tan skin. His white

shorts hung below his bony knees. He looked confused.

"Man, things are tweaked in this town," he said,
scratching the stubble on his face. "I'm used to people
knocking on the front door, not hopping the fence to
knock on the back one."

"Actually, most people use the front door here
too," I said, keeping my eyes on the gate. I explained
why I was avoiding Crusher.

"In that case, you can hide behind my fence any
time." The man extended his hand. "To my friends,
I'm Rusty."

"Willie Plummet," I said. "So you're a surfer,
huh?"

He nodded. "I learned to surf when I was 8 years
old and have been riding waves ever since. Before
coming here, I lived close enough to the beach to hear
the waves crashing outside my door."

"So why'd you move to Glenfield?" I asked.

"My work transferred me. It was either move or
lose my job."

I told him about the contest at Tidal Wave and
why I was so desperate to find a surfboard.

Rusty hardly let me finish before moving past me
to the side of the house. His thongs flapped with each
step. "As you can see, I'm still unpacking." He gave
the stuffed shark a light pat. "Mako here will go above
the fireplace when I'm done."

"That's so cool," I said, totally amazed. "But keep him away from Crusher or Mako may end up with an unwanted set of initials."

"Thanks for the tip," Rusty said. He opened the side door to the garage and pulled out the surfboard I'd noticed earlier. "This is yours if you want it. Other than a few dings, it's a good stick to learn on. And you can't beat the price."

"How much?" I asked.

"Free."

"Are you serious? Thanks! This is awesome." The surfboard was about seven feet tall and ivory colored. It had a few decals on the bottom—one of a wave, the other of a dolphin. I could tell the board wasn't in perfect shape, but it looked fine to me. "If you want this back when Tidal Wave opens, just let me know."

"Forget it," he said. "I've got other boards. That one is yours to keep."

I thanked Rusty again. After a quick check for Crusher, I opened the gate to leave.

Rusty followed me into the front yard. "Well, I hope you can learn to handle that board in time for the contest. Five weeks isn't much time to learn, but if there's anything I can do, just let me know."

"As a matter of fact, there is," I said, not sure if I should have brought it up. Rusty had been so generous already. But with Crusher moving in for the kill, I needed all the help I could get. God had certainly led me to a surfboard. Maybe He'd lead me to a surfing coach too. I explained my plan to have Orville pull me behind the Wave Ruler XT.

"That could help," Rusty said with a nod. "If I can swing it, I'll meet you at Lunker Lake on Saturday."

"That would be great," I said. On the way home, I could have surfed the air, I was walking so high. I thanked God with every step.

As soon as I got home, I showed Amanda and Orville my new surfboard. Unfortunately, their enthusiasm left a lot to be desired.

"Are you sure this thing will float?" Amanda asked.

"Good question," Orville added. "This thing has more holes than a pound of Swiss cheese."

"Knock it off, you guys," I told them. "This board rips, and so will I once I get the hang of it."

"*Rips* is right," Amanda cringed. "But is fiberglass supposed to be this torn up?"

Orville let out a laugh. "Little bro, all I've got to say is, wear a life vest."

To overcome their doubts, I quickly stacked two couch cushions on the floor and placed the surfboard on top of them. Lying down, I pretended like I was paddling.

Amanda rolled her eyes. "This is too much."

"My wave," I called out. I jumped to my feet. The cushions shifted and the surfboard titled in all directions. I pushed the nose down, lifted up, and rocked from side to side. With my knees bent slightly, I steadied my hands as if to keep balance on a giant wave.

Amanda and Orville let out a laugh, no doubt shocked by my ability.

"He pulls into the tube," I said, crouching down. "The fans go wild. They rise to their feet chanting, 'Plummet! Plummet!' "

"But Willie, the surfer-wannabe, can barely hear them," Orville added, picking up a pillow, "because the curl begins to break over his red head."

Whomp! Orville connected with the pillow, but I didn't fall. When he swung again, I ducked just in time.

"The kid is amazing," I went on. "Crouching so low, even the curl can't get him."

"Or so he thinks," Amanda said. She picked up a pillow and started swinging too. *Whomp*!

I leaned and bent but didn't fall. By shifting my weight to adjust for the blows, I remained on the board. "Plummet is unstoppable!" I yelled. "He can surf a hurricane and not fall."

"But not a typhoon," Orville said.

Whomp! Whomp! Thump! Thud! Orville and Amanda gave it their all.

Realizing the end was near, I did what any quick thinking little brother would do. I decided to take Amanda and Orville down with me. "Having won the contest, Plummet jumps from his board!" I declared.

Lunging out, I grabbed Amanda with one arm and Orville with the other. The three of us tumbled to the ground … and kept tumbling, right into the end table. The lamp on the table teetered for a moment, then fell over.

"What was that?" Mom asked, coming down the stairs.

Amanda and Orville glared in my direction without saying a thing.

I just shook my head. "Big wave, Mom. Typhoon big."

We were still on the floor when Dad came in the house. He wasn't happy about the lamp, but since all that broke was the bulb, he let us off easy. He mainly wanted to hear how I came across a surfboard. I gladly told him everything.

"What was the guy's name again?" Dad asked.

"Rusty. You should see all the cool stuff he has from the beach."

"I'd like to sometime," Dad said. "Right now my main concern is this surfboard. It has a lot of dings that need patching. But not to worry. I have some epoxy at the hobby store that should do the trick."

"Epoxy?" I asked. That scared me. Dad has every glue known to humanity. And he always goes overboard. He has a thing about models breaking. Whenever he supervises my work, his first comment is always, "Are you sure that's enough glue? Better add more just to be safe."

I pulled the board away from my dad. "That's okay. I can just duct tape the bad spots. That should do the trick. If not, I'll ask Rusty about it on Saturday."

"Willie, it's your board now, not Rusty's. You need to be responsible for its repair." Dad stepped over and pressed his fingers against one of the cracks on the deck. "Duct tape won't cut it on this crater. This board needs a good thick coat of epoxy resin. Maybe even two."

Oh, great, I thought. My board is going to weigh more than the *Titanic*. And we've all seen that movie. "Dad, I'm serious. You don't have to fix it."

"Willie, it's my pleasure. I've got to get back to the store after dinner. I'll work on it then."

"At least let me come with you, to help," I offered.

"Better not," he said. "I may be there late. And it's a school night."

"Yeah," Orville added, patting me on the head. "Little surfers need their rest."

"You stay out of this—until Saturday," I told him. "Then I'm counting on your truck, remember?"

Orville leaned close to me and whispered. "You'll need more than my truck when Dad gets through with that board. If I were you, I'd line up an 18-wheeler."

I sat silently as Dad carried my board to his van, fearing Orville was right.

Face Planting

By the time Saturday rolled around, the weight of my surfboard was only one of my concerns. Dad definitely had been generous in his use of epoxy, but at least all the cracks and dings were patched. Whether it was too heavy remained to be seen. And it was the *seen* part that bothered me.

Here's why. Sam, in her never-ending pursuit for interview experience, had arranged to tag along to Lunker Lake. She had convinced Felix to come too. I couldn't believe Felix was willing to give up a day at Tidal Wave. But he did, and he even borrowed a video camera to record my every move.

I would have told Sam and Felix no, but they got to Orville before me.

"Sounds like a great idea," he told them. "Every time Willie plants his face, we'll have it on film."

When we arrived at Lunker Lake, we got out and unloaded the surfboard, towels, and other gear. Then

Orville backed the truck to the edge of the lake, and lowered the Wave Ruler XT into the water.

"Now all we need is Rusty," I said, looking around. It occurred to me that a few words of advice would be nice before the camera started rolling.

"We're here at Lunker Lake with the self-proclaimed future surfing champion, Willie Plummet," Sam announced.

So much for a few words of advice. This time she held a real microphone and stared at the camera with its flashing red light.

"Willie, what's your strategy here today?" she asked, moving the mike to my face.

"I'll start off with the basics," I replied, trying to sound mellow yet confident, like surfers do. "I'll work on standing up and cutting and turning."

"Just so our viewers know, what's the difference between a cut and a turn?" Sam asked.

I bit my lip, staring at the camera. "Uh … I don't know. It just sounded good."

Orville laughed in the background. "Hey, bro, maybe you should stick with couch surfing."

"Well," Sam said, trying to regain the flow, "let's see how you do." With that Felix shut off the camera.

"Thanks a lot," I said. "Are you here to film surfing or to test my vocabulary?"

"Sorry. You know I'm not good at interviewing," Sam said, crossing her arms. "You're not the only one trying to learn something new."

"You're right, I forgot. Don't worry about it, Sam. Things will work out. Trust and delight, remember?"

"That's right," Felix added. "Psalm 37:3–4. I read it too."

After putting on his life vest, Orville took the Wave Ruler off shore to get the slack out of the ski rope.

"That's good," I shouted. Carrying the board to the edge of the water, I lay down and held the handle of the rope. The water was as warm and flat as an ironed blue shirt.

Felix waded knee deep into the lake to videotape the expression on my face as I shot past.

"Ready, Felix?" Sam asked.

"Sure. Go ahead and—ouch!" Felix stopped mid-sentence and splashed to shore. "Piranha! They're on the attack!"

"What?" I laughed. I floated to where he had been standing. Dozens of minnows darted back and forth. When I told Felix, he wouldn't believe me.

"Why would they come after me?"

"No offense," Sam said, "but it's probably your skin. It sort of stinks."

Felix shook his head. "You noticed too, huh? I've been using a special lotion just in case I get chicken pox. I hoped that no one would notice."

"Notice? I practically gagged on the way up here," I said. "But I just thought it was Orville's breath."

"I heard that," Orville shouted from out in the water. He revved the Wave Ruler a few times. "You're going to pay for that."

Once Felix washed off his legs and got set up again, it was time to find out what Orville had in mind.

"Go!" I yelled. Orville gunned the Wave Ruler, kicking up a rooster tail of water behind it.

The rope jerked me off the surfboard in one sudden motion. After 10 feet of playing human torpedo, I let go of the rope's handle and swam to the surface, coughing and hacking. The surfboard hadn't moved an inch, unlike the video camera, which had followed me every inch of the way. One look at the flashing red light and I wanted to dive down again, especially when I saw who had just arrived.

"That was some beginning," Rusty grinned.

"Tell me about it," I coughed.

Rusty took off his sandals and stepped into the water. "Looks like we got two problems here. One, the skags on the bottom of the surfboard were stuck in the sand. Two, you forgot to wax the deck. But don't sweat it. I came prepared."

Rusty removed a bar of surf wax from his pocket and rubbed it all over the board. "Now you're ready," he pronounced.

This time I started farther out and told Orville not to gun it so hard.

"Ready?" Orville asked.

"Go for it!" I shouted.

Orville moved ahead until the rope grew taut. After the initial jerk, the board took off with me on top. I skimmed across the water with ease. Now all I had to do was stand up. Clutching the rope's handle with one hand, I used the other to push myself up— first to my knees, then to my feet.

"Yes! I'm doing it!" I shouted to Rusty and the others on shore.

Rusty responded with a thumbs up.

I responded with the same sign. Too bad Orville took that to mean go faster. He punched the Wave Ruler XT like he was going for the checkered flag.

I launched over the board and hit the water like a bug hits a windshield. By the time I surfaced, the surfboard came zooming up from behind and whacked me on the head.

"Was that fast enough?" Orville asked, cruising up.

"Almost. A little faster and I could have flown all the way to the ocean. Then I could have surfed real waves instead of relying on you," I grumbled.

We got set up again and Orville pulled me along. This time rising to my feet came easier. Cruising across the surface, I felt confident enough to hold the rope with one hand and wave to the people on shore. My experience with water-skiing and snowboarding was definitely paying off when it came to balance.

Pretty soon we reached the end of the lake and Orville turned back. Unfortunately, I didn't. The surfboard kept going straight. It occurred to me that

Rusty hadn't told me how to turn. I decided it had to be about leaning.

Because Orville was turning to the left, I decided to lean in the same direction. Too bad the board didn't cooperate.

Splat! I hit the water hard with a world-class belly flop and swallowed a gallon of lake water. The board kept going, straight for a woman sunbathing on an inflatable mattress. People probably heard the pop in town when the nose of the surfboard pierced the plastic. Down she went. I'm not sure a torpedo could have sunk her any quicker.

Orville pulled the Wave Ruler around. "That was smooth, bro. You must be a future surf champion."

After 10 minutes of apologizing and promising to pay the woman for the repair, we finally got started again. Unfortunately, the results were the same. I splashed down on one side, then the other. Every time I leaned, the board didn't. By the time we returned to the others on the beach, I felt like calling it quits.

"That problem with the air mattress was my fault," Rusty said. "I should have given you a leash with the board. Wait here a minute." He ran to his van and returned with a black leash.

"I think I need more than a leash," I muttered.

"Take it easy," Rusty told me. He attached the leash to the surfboard. "You'll get it. The secret to turning is placing your back foot near the end of the board, directly above the skags. If you put all your weight on that foot, you can pivot the board on a dime."

"That doesn't sound too hard," Sam said. "Let me give it a try."

"Be my guest," I said with a laugh, eager to see a face other than my own planted in the water.

Too bad that's not what happened. Once Orville got her going, Sam got right up and cruised along. She even turned back and forth across the wake. After a few trips around the lake, she brought it in.

"Don't take it too hard, bro," Rusty said. He patted me on the shoulder. "While you were out there learning the hard way, I taught her what you were doing right and wrong. That means every time you wiped out, Sam was learning a little more about surfing."

"Thanks, that makes me feel s-o-o-o-o much better," I muttered.

Rusty laughed. "Trust me, Willie. You'll get it."

He was right. When I got back on the board, I picked up on turning. By the time we had to leave, I wasn't just cutting across the wake, I was banking off of it and even trying a few jumps. In fact, I was so stoked on my progress, I couldn't wait to see the videotape of me in action.

After saying good-bye to Rusty, we packed everything up and headed home.

"So where should we watch the tape?" I asked.

"Sorry, Willie. You can't watch it," Sam said. "I've got to get it to the station immediately."

"No way," I objected.

"Willie, this is great stuff, not just of you surfing, but of my interview with Rusty," Sam explained. "When the news director sees this, I'm bound to be assigned to the surf contest at Tidal Wave."

"But what about the footage of me wiping out?" I asked. "He'll laugh his head off when he sees that."

"I know I did," Orville added.

"Me too," Felix followed. "You don't know how hard it is to hold a camera still when you're cracking up. Today I was hysterically challenged."

I glared at Sam. "See what I mean?"

"Willie, no offense, but the director has more important things to do than watch videos of you learning to surf," Sam reasoned. "I just want him to see that I'm improving. Besides, what's the worst that can happen? He laughs at you falling? People laugh at you all the time. Big deal."

"When you put it that way, I feel *way* better," I announced, my voice dripping with sarcasm.

Sam put her arm across my shoulder. "That's what friends are for."

The rest of the way home, I felt sick. Something told me that the director laughing wasn't even close to the worst that could happen.

And, boy, was I right.

⑨

Surf Chump

A little after five, Sam called my house. "Willie, good news. The director loved the video footage we shot today. He says I'm definitely improving as a reporter."

"Way to go, Sam," I said, glad to hear things had worked out.

"He said he might even use some of the footage tonight. It all depends on how long the sports segment takes," she announced.

Suddenly, my gladness turned to mourning. "What do you mean, tonight? I hope you told him what shots he could and could not include."

"Yeah, right, I'm supposed to tell the *director* what to do," Sam said.

"You could have at least tried."

"Willie, how bad could it be?" Sam asked. "By the time we finished, you were surfing awesome. Now quit whining and turn on the TV. That's what I'm going to do. Bye."

After hanging up, I ran over and flipped on the TV. Susan Hunter finished a segment on inflation with, "When we come back, our teen reporter, Samantha Stewart, follows spring training for a self-proclaimed surf champion."

"Did I hear that right?" Dad asked, lowering his paper.

"Yep. You sure did."

Standing up, Dad called everyone into the family room.

"I hope they got my good side," Orville said.

"This is so exciting," Amanda bubbled. "My baby brother is going to be on TV."

"Brother, yes. Baby, no," I informed her, feeling confident. "And this is just the beginning. Wait until I win that contest."

When the commercials ended, the camera returned to Susan Hunter, who quickly introduced the video clip. Then the image cut to the shot of Sam interviewing me just before I got on the surfboard.

"There I am," I said. "So far so good."

If only it had remained that way. The next shot showed me lying on the surfboard and being launched into the water. From there, the clip cut to Orville gunning the Wave Ruler and my face plant. To make things worse, it showed the same scene again in slow motion.

"That's hilarious," Orville announced with a laugh.

I heard Amanda and Mom busting up too.

The next clip showed me doing the belly flop when I turned and the board didn't. But that wasn't all. The video immediately went to a shot of me falling on my back. Then both clips ran together again and again and again. It looked like the surfboard had me by the feet and was slapping me back and forth on the water like some kind of aqua puppet. Back and forth. Back and forth.

Dad was laughing so hard he dropped to his knees. The rest of the family followed suit, clutching their sides and wiping their eyes.

"What's so funny?" I fumed.

When Susan Hunter came on again, even she was laughing. "Well, I guess we all have to start somewhere," she chuckled. "Apparently the road from surf chump to surf champ is harder than it seems."

"That's it!" I shouted. Marching over, I shut off the TV and left the room.

"Are you sure that wasn't *America's Funniest Home Videos*?" Orville called after me.

I didn't honor his wisecrack with a response. Instead, I headed to the solitude of my room, determined not to speak to anyone else the whole night.

Unfortunately, I had only maintained my promise of silence for 10 minutes when the phone rang.

"Willie, it's for you," Mom called up the stairs.

"I'm not home," I replied.

"Is that what you want me to tell Rusty?" she asked.

Rusty? I jumped off my bed and ran downstairs to the phone. "What's up?" I asked, out of breath. "Don't tell me you saw the news?"

"I did, dude. Talk about a bummer. Just watching it stressed me out," he answered.

"Why, because it made me look so bad?"

"No, because I kept thinking they would introduce me as your coach. That would have killed me," Rusty explained.

"Glad you avoided the pain," I said sarcastically.

Rusty let a moment of silence go by before speaking. "Willie, you've got to lighten up. I was just kidding. Besides, I think I came up with an idea that will take you to the next level."

"The next level?"

"That's right. By the end of the day you were surfing awesome," Rusty said. "But there's one slight problem."

"Go ahead. I can take it."

"You were pulled. When you surf, the speed comes from the board on the water, not from someone pulling you."

"But that's because there's a wave. Until the park is completed, I don't have a wave. I have six-inch wakes," I replied.

"Then find another way to keep moving," Rusty said. "Just make sure you're not pulled and your hands are free. When you come up with something, stop by and we'll go for lesson number 2. Talk to you later, dude. Aloha." With that Rusty hung up.

He'd said he had an *idea*. That was no idea. That was a problem. I climbed back upstairs to my room, wishing I hadn't taken the call in the first place.

The next day at church, I met up with Sam and Felix in the parking lot before the service.

"That was some news clip," Felix said with a smile. "One look at that and *America's Funniest Home Videos* will make you their all-time champion."

"That's a good idea," Sam added. "That way if you don't win the surf contest, you'll have something to fall back on."

"Not funny," I said, my face downcast. I filled them in on my conversation with Rusty. "Why is it that every time I think things are going my way, something goes wrong?"

Felix slugged me in the arm. "Listen to you. Aren't you the one who told us to trust in the Lord?"

"I'm trying," I said. "But it's not easy."

During the sermon, I did my best to stay focused, but my mind kept wandering to the surf contest. I felt guilty worrying. I knew I could trust God, but it was hard. I wanted to win so badly. It was the desire of my heart. But how could I make sure it would happen?

Then an amazing thing happened. The pastor made a reference to the exact same verses in Psalm 37 that I'd been thinking about. He explained that God has promised to give us what we need, like food and clothes, but especially the gift of faith. He knows what will make us happy and what will hurt us. God will answer our prayers according to His plan for our lives.

I thought of all the people in the Bible whom God had done incredible things for—Noah, Abraham, David, the people Jesus healed. They had trusted God to do the right thing and He had done even better things for them. What did I have to worry about?

"Okay, Lord," I whispered in prayer. "I get the point." After church I told Sam and Felix what had happened.

"What'd I tell you?" Felix said.

We were still talking when a surprised voice came from behind me. "Willie, is that you?"

I turned to see Rusty walking my way. With his Hawaiian shirt and sandals, he didn't exactly fit in with the rest of us.

"Yep," I said. "Is this your first time here?"

"Yeah, but not my last. The service was great, and everyone has made me feel welcome."

"Cool," I said, thankful that Rusty wasn't judged because of his clothes. That's how it ought to be.

After saying hello to Felix and Sam, Rusty returned his attention to me. "I'm a little surprised to see you here."

"Why? I've been coming here for years," I said.

"Really? That's good," Rusty replied. He intentionally avoided my eyes.

"What is it?" I persisted.

"If I tell you, can I still be your coach?" he asked.

"Sure."

"You stress out too much, especially for a Christian," Rusty said. "The Lord will work things out. You know that. Things may not go exactly how you want them to, but God will take care of you either way."

I bit my lip and glanced at Sam and Felix. Felix told Rusty about the verses I had read in Psalm 37.

"Sounds like you're getting it from all sides," Rusty said.

"Yeah," I said. "But you won't hear me complain. I need it."

"So do I," Sam added. She explained that she still hadn't landed the internship as a teen reporter.

"That doesn't make sense," I fumed. "They loved what you brought them from Lunker Lake. It sounds like you're getting the runaround to me, Sam. Maybe

I should call the station manager and put in a good word for you."

"That's okay, Willie," Sam insisted quickly.

"I'm serious," I went on. "I'd be happy to go to bat for you."

"No need."

"Really. Just give me the word and I'm on the phone," I persisted.

"Please. I'm begging you, Willie," Sam pleaded. "Keep out of this."

I lifted my hands in defeat. "Suit yourself. I was just trying to help."

Felix was next to complain. He told Rusty about the stress involved with the remodeling of Tidal Wave.

"At least you don't smell like some stinky lotion anymore," I joked.

"Laugh all you want. But I don't have chicken pox, do I?" Felix replied. Then he snuck a quick glance at his arms. "At least not yet."

"Sounds like trust is an issue for all of you," Rusty said. "But don't worry, the Lord will work things out."

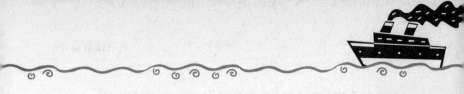

The SurfMaster 1000

Although my trust level went up, my hopes of winning the contest didn't. By Wednesday, I was beginning to feel like a wave in the wind, tossed back and forth by doubt.

In desperation I decided to take the surfboard to the lab in the storeroom of Plummet's Hobbies. I placed it on the operating table, then I stood back and stared at it, hoping for a flash of inspiration.

All I got was the flash of Orville's white teeth. He smiled every time he came back to do a stock check. "Interesting technique, Willie. Why solve your problems when you can just stare them away?"

"Real funny. Thanks for being so helpful," I said.

"I told you my idea. You wouldn't take it," Orville said, returning to the front of the store.

I shook my head in frustration. Orville's idea was to make the surfboard self-powered. At first that sounded great. I even called Rusty to get permission to modify the board he had given to me.

"Do whatever you want to it," was his response. "It's your board now, not mine."

At that point I was ready to go, and would have, if I could have come up with the right means. But the model engines in the store weren't powerful enough. And a boat engine, like the one in the Wave Ruler XT, would be too heavy. After talking it over with Felix and Sam, and even my dad, I finally dropped the idea. As much as I wanted a self-powered surfboard, I just couldn't figure out how to pull it off.

"How's it going?" Felix asked, entering the lab.

"Not good," I said, my eyes fixed on the board.

"Orville looked happy enough," Felix commented.

"Don't remind me."

"In the mood for a present?" Felix asked.

"Not unless it's the world's smallest jet engine," I scoffed.

"Who told you?" Felix removed the box from under his arm and put it on the surfboard. "Take a look."

I opened the box and pulled out a small engine. It couldn't have weighed more than 10 pounds, including the battery pack attached to it. "Where'd you get this?"

"At Tidal Wave. It powered Happy the Hammerhead," Felix explained. "Remember how it always swam around in that pool?"

"Yeah, it was the lamest thing at the park. Crusher's initials in Happy's hide didn't help either."

"Exactly," Felix said, adjusting his glasses. "That's why Happy got the boot and you get the engine. It was custom-made to be one of the most powerful compact jet engines in existence."

"This is awesome. I hate to gloat over Happy's untimely death, but this is totally awesome!" I exclaimed.

Hearing my enthusiasm, Dad and Orville came into the lab. They were quick to see the potential of Felix's contribution.

"What'd I tell you?" Orville said. "A self-powered surfboard."

The three of us got to work right away. Dad even got into the act, as long as there wasn't a customer in the store. We agreed to position the engine just in front of the skags on the bottom of the surfboard. Although half of the engine fit in the board, the other half hung below it.

"Not a problem," Dad said. He climbed a ladder and removed an old box from the highest shelf. It was full of balsa wood scraps he had collected over the years. "We'll use these scraps to make an engine compartment. At the most, it will hang down two inches below the bottom of the surfboard."

"That's nothing," I said. "The skags hang four inches below the bottom."

"Exactly," Dad explained. "The thrust of the jets will shoot from the back of the compartment, right past the skags."

"Are you sure foam and balsa wood are strong enough to hold this engine?" Orville asked.

"With extra fiberglass and resin, it should be fine," Felix said.

"And don't forget the epoxy Dad put on already. This thing is strong as a tank," I reminded everyone.

For the next several hours, we cut, shaped, and sanded balsa wood until the compartment was ready. Then we put a layer of fiberglass and epoxy over the whole thing. Once it dried, we applied another layer, then another.

Dad called Mom to tell her we wouldn't be home for dinner. Then he ordered pizza so we could work into the evening. By the time the board was done, we all stood back in awe. From the top, it looked like a regular surfboard. Inside and underneath, a low-profile jet engine was ready to go to work.

"Everyone," I announced, "say hello to the Surf-Master 1000." A round of applause followed.

"What do you think, Orville? Can I get a ride to Lunker Lake tomorrow after school?" I asked.

"You got it," he said.

I was so excited about what we had accomplished that I called Rusty.

He was just as enthusiastic. "I'll get off early from work and see you at the lake," he said. "It's time for lesson 2 on the way to become a surf champion. What'd I tell you about trust?"

"I've learned my lesson," I said, eager to get to Lunker Lake and see what the SurfMaster 1000 could do. And this time, no video cameras.

After easing the SurfMaster into Lunker Lake, I paddled out to deep water. At first I was concerned about the added weight from the jet engine and the compartment that hung below the board. What if the board moved through the water like a refrigerator?

Fortunately, my fears were soon put to rest. The engine compartment wasn't a problem at all. The drag was practically non-existent. I looked back at the shore for a little support from Rusty.

"You can do it, dude," he called out. His confidence in me really helped. Before I paddled out, he had looked over the SurfMaster 1000 and was totally impressed. "The balsa wood covered with epoxy is the perfect combination. You've got lightweight and plenty of strength. I can't wait to see how this handles."

"Well, here it goes," I muttered.

I paddled as hard as I could. I dug deep with my arms, stroking the water. As the board skipped across the lake, I hit the power button on the engine. Even at low speed, the board picked up the pace. Pretty soon I was moving so well that I stopped paddling.

At first I didn't want to stand up. It was cool gliding across the water on my belly. To turn right, I leaned to the right. To turn left, I leaned to the left. Piece of cake. I made a big circle and cruised by everyone on shore. They stood knee deep in the water, laughing and waving as I sped past. They were having as much fun watching as I was having riding the SurfMaster.

Talk about an awesome invention! This wasn't just a SurfMaster. This was a SurfMasterpiece! And I was just getting warmed up.

Returning my hands to the water, I paddled hard, just like I would to catch a wave.

"Make your move, dude!" Rusty called out.

Bringing my hands to the sides of the board, I pushed up hard. Then, in one quick motion, I brought my feet underneath me. They stuck in the fresh wax. Now all I had to do was let go of the sides of the board and straighten up. *Not a problem*, I thought. I'd done it the other day when Orville was pulling me with the Wave Ruler XT. Why couldn't I do it now?

For some reason, I couldn't bring myself to let go. My hands felt more stuck than my feet.

"Let go and stand up," Orville shouted, "or I'll swim out there and show you how it's done."

"Yeah, right," I laughed.

The crazy thing is, I knew Orville meant it, which turned out to be just the motivation I needed.

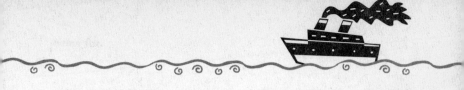

Feet on Fiberglass

I let go of the sides of the SurfMaster and began to straighten my legs. I wobbled higher and higher, extending my hands like a tightrope walker.

"It's working," I shouted. "I'm not water-skiing on a surfboard, I'm really *surfing*!" Claps and cheers echoed across the water from the shore.

I decided to try high speed. When I moved my foot to hit the *High* button, I almost lost my balance. The safest bet would be to crouch down and hit the button with my hand. If needed, I could grab the sides again.

But since when was the safest way the Willie Plummet way?

No respectable surfer would use his hands to make an adjustment, especially not a soon-to-be surf champion. Surfing was all about feet on fiberglass. I'd seen clips of surfers actually walking up and down their boards. If they could do that, I could at least

move my foot a few inches to hit an acceleration button.

"Surf's up," I shouted with determination. I lifted
my foot and brought it down on *High.*

And believe me, I went high. The SurfMaster
launched out from under me like a missile. I landed
with a splash, the hard water stinging my bare back.
Good thing I had a leash. Or so I thought. When the
slack pulled tight, I felt like a cowboy on a runaway
horse with one boot caught in a stirrup.

We had forgotten one small detail when planning
the SurfMaster 1000. We knew the leash would keep
the board from getting away, but we never figured out
how I would climb back on. Flailing at the water, I
gasped for air. I had to do something fast. Bending
forward, I grabbed the leash around my ankle and
pulled myself toward the SurfMaster. It felt like I was
crawling through a downhill current.

Then suddenly it stopped.

I looked up to see Rusty sitting on the SurfMaster.
His hand was still pressing the *Stop* button. "Good
thing you were heading our way. Normally surfers
don't wear life vests, but maybe in your case—"

"No thanks," I interrupted. "There's no need for
that."

"I'm just kidding, bro. You got up on the first try.
Nobody does that. So what if you fell? That's just part
of surfing."

Hearing Rusty encouraged me. I decided to quit being so uptight. I also decided to let him have a try. By the way he was looking at the SurfMaster and pushing his hands on the wax, I could tell he really wanted to have a surfboard under his feet again.

"I'd love to try a few moves," he said.

By the time I swam to shore, Rusty was on his feet and in high speed. With his left foot forward and his right foot all the way to the back of the board, he turned like a pro. And every turn was different. Some were sharp slashes that sent a fan of spray into the air. Others were gradual bends.

When he brought the SurfMaster around and headed toward shore, a smile spread across his tan face. "I've never been so happy and so sad at the same time," he told us. "Happy for the chance to try out such an awesome invention. But sad for how much I miss the ocean."

"Well, hang in there for another four weeks and Tidal Wave will be at your service," Felix said.

"Thanks for the offer, Felix. It won't be the same, but it'll have to do." Rusty handed me the SurfMaster. "The jump to high speed isn't as bad as it seems. Just lean forward and you'll be okay."

With the SurfMaster beneath me, I paddled out and took Rusty's advice. And just like before, I flew off the back and smacked the water. But this time I worked my way back to the board and climbed to my feet.

Although it was a little intimidating at first, high speed actually made turning the SurfMaster easier. Low speed felt like turning really slowly on a bike— you always have that fear that you're going to fall over. But high speed was smooth. After just a short while, I was cutting grooves in the water as I turned one way, then the next. With my back foot on the tail of the board, I pivoted the nose around and even slapped it up and down like you would bunny hop a skateboard. *Now this is the kind of day you video-tape*, I thought. Where's Felix when I need him?

The applause from the shore encouraged me more. I leaned heavily on my back foot and whipped the nose around, sending a small fan of spray through the air.

"You can do better than that," Rusty shouted.

Enough said. I was up for the challenge. The key was more speed. Keeping the board straight, I zoomed to the other side of the lake. With the wind at my back, I really moved.

Crouching slightly, I braced myself for the hard lean. But my focus was so heavily on improving my next turn that I didn't notice the person in front of me.

Someone on a surfboard was being pulled behind a Jet Ski. That made sense. They probably had seen me on the news and decided to give it a try. Whoever it was obviously had his eye on the surf contest and had come to Lunker Lake to practice.

And he needed it. When he hit a little ripple, he sprawled into the water. At first I panicked because I was headed right for him. Then I realized that avoiding him would be easy, if that was really what I wanted to do. But why not spray him instead? That's the least he deserved for copying my idea.

"Surf that!" I yelled, slicing a giant rainbow of water onto his head. I pulled away, laughing, only to hear the surfer-wannabe screaming my name. Crusher Grubb clung to his surfboard, coughing to clear his lungs.

"You're mine, Plummet," he shouted.

Why me? I thought. Every time I try to have a little fun, it backfires. Fortunately, Crusher didn't bother to come after me. For once he was more concerned about getting practice than getting even.

Fearing that the SurfMaster's batteries might run low, I sped across the lake to join up with the others. I wanted to make sure enough power remained for Orville and Sam to have a turn.

I was glad I gave them the opportunity. We all laughed as they struggled to paddle, stand, and turn. Sam went first, followed by Orville. All the while Rusty used them as examples to teach me more about surfing. It was also then that he told me to consider another idea.

"Rusty, no offense, but your last idea turned out to be a problem," I reminded him.

"A problem? I thought you were learning to trust and not doubt." Rusty directed my attention across the water. "What do you see?"

"Lunker Lake."

"Anything about it stand out in your mind?" he asked.

"It's wet."

"Keep going," Rusty prompted.

"It's not dry."

Rusty dropped his shoulders in frustration. "It's flat. You dig? As flat as flat gets. No swells, no peaks, no barrels."

"Why did I know the victory of this moment wouldn't last?" I said.

"Better you face facts now than on the day of the contest. You need water with some slope to it," Rusty said. "Surfing is based on the fact that water *isn't* always flat. Sometimes it's at a slight angle; other times it's vertical. And once in a great while, if the Lord is really good to you, it forms a curling ceiling over your head."

"You mean a barrel?" I asked.

He nodded with conviction. "A barrel."

Sitting down on the tailgate of Orville's truck, I dropped my head. "Where am I supposed to find vertical water? You haven't seen any lying around, have you?"

Rusty slapped me on the shoulder before walking away. "Trust Him, Willie. You've got to trust Him. Aloha." With that he got into his car and drove away.

I was still staring at the ground when Felix came over and sat next to me.

"I may have a solution to your problem, Willie," Felix said. "It's not available yet, so I don't want to get your hopes up."

"When will it be available?"

"A month or so," Felix said. "Don't stress over it. You may not want anything to do with it when you find out what it is."

"After today I'm ready for anything," I announced, never thinking that my response would later be classified under *famous last words*.

For the next month I searched for sloped water but came up empty. Since Felix's idea still hadn't worked out either, I kept surfing Lunker Lake with the SurfMaster 1000. Even though the water was flat, I wanted to get as confident as I could with a board under my feet.

The remodeling at Tidal Wave continued to move ahead with amazing speed. God really blessed Mr. Patterson, especially since he kept losing employees to chicken pox. I couldn't believe so many adults had never had them as kids.

The surf community was getting excited about the idea of a surf contest at a water park. One of their frustrations with contests had always been the quality of the waves. Sometimes the sets were almost unrideable because they were so small. The pros wanted medium to big waves with good shape. That meant hollow faces, peaks, and plenty of peel along the shoulder. That way they could pull off one hot move after another.

According to Mr. Patterson, Pipeline Lagoon would offer just the right waves and plenty of them.

With all the renovations and contest decorations coming together, I couldn't wait to get out to Tidal Wave. But Felix kept me away, coming up with one excuse after another.

With the contest only a week away, it looked like I wouldn't get to see the place until opening day. Then one Friday night Felix surprised me.

"Willie, phone's for you," Mom said.

Felix greeted me with two words. "We're ready."

"What do you mean?"

"Tomorrow morning at Tidal Wave. We're ready for our test engineer to pay a visit. And bring the Surf-Master 1000. You'll need it." Felix hung up without offering any more information.

No need to stress over it, I told myself. *Trust in the Lord. You'll know soon enough what's going on.*

Flash Flood

Rusty gave Sam and me a ride to Tidal Wave the next morning. The receptionist told us that we could find Felix at Big Niagara. Wandering through the park, I could see that Rusty was impressed.

"This place is something," he said. "I feel like I'm back in Hawaii."

Palm trees lined the walkways between rides. Tropical plants with big green leaves and bright flowers dotted the landscape.

"It looks like they could open today," I said. With the SurfMaster 1000 jammed under my arm, I felt increasingly jazzed about Felix's plan. If only I knew what it was.

"There he is," Sam said and pointed.

Felix stood at the top of Big Niagara, talking to one of the workers. When he saw us, he ran toward us. That's when I noticed something on his face. It looked like a surgeon's mask.

"Is that what I think it is?" I asked Sam.

"Beats me," she replied.

It was.

"Ut cook goo oh long?" Felix mumbled as he approached us.

"I have no idea what you said," I told him. "What's with the mask?"

Felix stopped a ways from us and lifted the mask from his mouth. "Chicken pox prevention. Now, what took you so long?"

"It was my fault," Rusty admitted. "We had to wait for the battery to charge in my video camera."

"I tried to talk him out of bringing it," I explained. "But Sam seems to think everything I do is headline news. I guess that's just the price of being a future surf legend."

"Evidently," Felix quipped. "But seriously, are you ready for some water with a little slope to it?"

"Only for the last month," I said with anticipation. Although Felix had yet to reveal his plan, in my mind it could only mean one place: Pipeline Lagoon. The wave machine was obviously ready, and it was time for Tidal Wave's test engineer to try it out.

"In that case—"

"Felix! Can you give me a hand up here," a worker shouted from the top of Big Niagara. "Pronto!"

"Gotta go," Felix said. Without hesitation he returned the mask to his face and took off.

"What about the sloped water?" I shouted after him.

"Blash Fud!" he shouted through the mask.

"What kind of ride is *Blash Fud*?" Rusty asked.

Sam already had figured it out. "You don't think he meant—"

"Unreal," I gasped. "Of all the rides with sloped water, Felix sends me to that one."

"What?" Rusty asked.

I silently led Sam and Rusty across the park to a mountain of rocks with a narrow gorge. It twisted and fell from the mountain's peak to ground level. As we approached, the sound of rushing water grew louder, like a dam had burst.

At the base of the mountain, where the line would begin, a sign read: FLASH FLOOD: *Ride at your own risk!*

"No question about it. This water is definitely sloped," Rusty admitted.

We watched the white torrent as it sloshed around vertical banks, rose and fell over bumps, and tumbled down steep inclines. The ride ended with a waterfall that dumped into the receiving pool at the bottom.

After giving Rusty the cue, Sam produced a microphone and started the interview. "We're here with Willie Plummet, self-professed surf superstar, as he prepares to surf Flash Flood in preparation for Saturday's contest."

I flexed my muscles for the camera. "Can you see all of me? I hope that's a wide-angle lens."

Sam cleared her throat and went on. "Willie, I understand you're Tidal Wave's test engineer. That's some title. How did you get it?"

"Well, I've been around water all my life," I responded.

"Meaning?"

I glared at Sam for putting me on the spot. "Um … you know … baths, showers. That sort of thing."

"That's certainly impressive," Sam replied. "Willie, let's talk strategy. What can we look for on this ride?"

"Body parts," I said, swallowing hard.

Sam chuckled and winked at the camera. "Well, folks, Willie's sense of humor is still intact. We'll find out about the rest of him when he gets through with the mountain."

I never walked so slowly in my life. The SurfMaster 1000 felt more like a casket than a brilliant invention. At the top of the mountain, Flash Flood looked even deadlier. No wonder the sign read "Ride at your own risk." At least lying down I would be safe in the half pipes that formed the narrow gorge. Standing up would expose me to everything.

Sam and Rusty apparently were concerned about the same thing because they had moved away from me and were mumbling between themselves.

"Willie," Rusty said, "Flash Flood may be sloped, but it's not what I had in mind. Trying to keep a surfboard under control down this water would be next to impossible."

Here it comes, I thought, *they're going to beg me to reconsider.* "I know what you're getting at. You want me to call it off, right?"

"No. I want you to take it in high speed," Rusty said. "If you're going to keep control, you need to move even faster than the water itself."

"Faster?" I gasped. "If I do that, I'll launch myself halfway across the park."

"Easy now. This is no time to show off. Remember, you're here to practice." With that Rusty placed the SurfMaster in the water at the start of the ride. The rushing current pulled so hard, he had to strain to hang on.

I took off my shirt and climbed onto the board, belly down. I could see Sam speaking into the camera, saying something I couldn't distinguish. I knew I'd regret it at broadcast time.

"Ready?" Rusty shouted.

I clung to the side of the board as the cool water splashed over me. "No!"

For some reason he took that to mean yes. He hit the power button on the SurfMaster and shoved me off.

I launched through the white water, getting tossed from side to side. The SurfMaster bounced atop the raging current. It was all I could do to hang on. At first the thought of trying to stand up made me sick. I just wanted to survive. Then that verse came to mind.

"Trust in the Lord!" I shouted just before a splash of water filled my mouth.

Squeezing the sides of the board, I pushed up and swung my feet underneath me in one fluid motion. But surfing Flash Flood was nothing like surfing Lunker Lake. I struggled just to stay on my feet. The water dipped and rose like a roller coaster. *At least I'm still in low speed,* I thought. *Sure.*

To keep my balance, I repositioned my feet and accidentally stepped on the *High* button. The board shot forward and I had to cling to the back to keep from falling off. Suddenly, a quick left appeared. The SurfMaster slashed through a vertical wall of water. I dug in hard and made it.

"Yes!" I hollered. "That's what a sloped turn is all about."

At the next drop, I caught air and landed on a peak of white water. The current sloshed back and forth. My arms jerked in spastic response to the tumbling foam. Flash Flood poured down one chute after another. Water splashed from side to side. But I stayed agile on my feet and the SurfMaster handled it well.

I glanced back to see Rusty's response. He clapped and cheered. Seeing that he was impressed made me feel great. Not seeing the next slope wasn't so great. The SurfMaster dropped so fast, I almost fell over the nose. The slope just kept going, plunging down in what felt like a vertical drop. So much for flat water, I decided. It was all I could do to stay on my feet, but somehow I managed.

Then I saw a massive left turn in front of me. The water rose high on the bank as it made the turn. The SurfMaster moved at the speed of light. Spray pelted my chest and face. I dug in as hard as I could with my back foot. It wasn't enough.

I launched over the bank like some kind of seaplane. I caught so much air that my great-great-grandfather, Jedediah Plummet, an aviation pioneer, would have been proud.

There was just one small problem, though. Landing. I had soared well beyond the perimeter of Flash Flood.

"Whoa!" I shouted. "Look out below."

I braced myself for the worst. For concrete. For boulders. For an iron fence topped with spikes. But what I got was … water.

Splash! The SurfMaster came down on a cushion of white water. I had flown far enough to actually reach an adjacent ride. The question was, which one? The water moved swiftly, through wider channels, but didn't have the roaring rapids feel to it.

"Yes!" I shouted in victory, raising my hands. "Put *that* jump on TV!" I knocked off a few sharp "S" turns in celebration.

As the river picked up speed, so did I. Slashing and turning, I sprayed the steep walls on each side of me with water. For fun, I dug deep and put a rooster tail over the wall.

I was just about to let out another cheer when an angry voice cut me off.

"Ey, wha zit!" a familiar voice shouted. Suddenly, Felix's head appeared on the other side of the embankment. He yanked off his mask, his eyes full of fear. "Willie, you did that? How'd you get in there?"

"Jumped! All the way from Flash Flood."

"Flash Flood? I told you to take Splash Fun, the kiddy ride. Flash Flood isn't even finished. You could have been killed!"

"Now you tell me," I yelled back. "Good thing I got out when I did."

Felix ran along the wall to keep up with me. "Willie, you jumped from the frying pan into the fire. You've got to get out of here too. Quick!"

"Relax. If I can handle Flash Flood, I can handle anything," I cranked a sharp turn, spraying Felix with water. "Where am I anyway?"

"Big Niagara!" Felix shouted. "The falls are just around the bend. But the pool at the bottom isn't full yet. If you go over, you're toast."

My cocky attitude sank in a hurry. "What do you mean, *not full*?"

"You'll drop 20 feet into six inches of water," Felix warned. He ran with me, puffing hard. "Give me your hand, quick!"

I hit the *Off* switch on the SurfMaster and checked to make sure the leash was tight around my ankle. Suddenly, it was almost impossible to keep my balance. It was like trying to sit on a stopped bike on a conveyor belt.

"Grab my hand!" Felix shouted.

I couldn't reach it. The sound of falls landing on concrete rose through the channel. I could see the end coming fast. The water picked up speed, sloshing off the walls.

"Now!" Felix begged.

Lunging from the board, I extended my arm. Felix leaned over the rail to catch me. Stretching as far as I could, I grabbed his hand. The SurfMaster flew out from under me and kept going. My body dropped in the water. The current dragged me down with the force of a garbage disposal.

"Hang on," Felix grunted.

I did. Too bad he didn't.

Felix let go of the rail and tumbled into the water on top of me. I should have seen it coming, since Felix isn't exactly the heaviest guy on earth.

When Felix surfaced, he went for my throat. "Way to go, surf star!"

"You're the one who fell over the rail," I shouted back.

We scraped at the sides, trying to stop ourselves, but it was no use. The current carried us downriver through growing rapids topped with foam. The end was in sight. Big Niagara loomed ever closer, eager to pour us into oblivion.

When we reached the edge, Felix and I clasped hands, friends to the end. Pouring over the top, it seemed like we would never land, like we were in one of those airplanes that drops water on a fire. To make things worse, I feared the SurfMaster would land just in front of me and I'd get skewered like a roast turkey.

Splat! I hit the shallow pool hard and rolled across the surface. When I opened my eyes, Felix was beside me on his back, staring up at the blue sky. He looked like he had just jumped from a plane without a parachute. Next to him, the SurfMaster 1000 floated in two pieces. But neither Felix nor I had any broken bones. I whispered a quick thank-You prayer.

"Have a nice trip?" I asked.

"No. That first step was a doosie," he replied.

Overcome with relief, I let out a laugh. "Thanks for trying to save my life, bro."

"Don't mention it," Felix said. "Just knowing you're okay makes up for the fact that every bone in my body is crushed."

"Your jaw seems to be working okay."

Just then Rusty and Sam came running up.

"You should have seen it," I said.

"Don't worry," Sam noted, patting the video camera. "We did."

Trouble in the Tropics

In the parking lot outside Tidal Wave, I had enough butterflies in my stomach to carry me away. The day of the Pro-Am Surf Contest had finally arrived. Rusty was supposed to meet me, but he still hadn't arrived. And from what I could tell, everyone else in the state already had.

Cars, vans, trucks, and even tour buses spread from one end of the parking lot to the other. Opening day had come, and the place was packed.

After what had happened last week, I found myself wishing this day *hadn't* come. With the Surf-Master 1000 in two pieces, I wasn't able to practice at all. For the last seven days I hadn't ridden on a surfboard once.

To make things worse, Sam's TV station played the video of me and Felix plunging over Big Niagara again and again. Of course they didn't use even one

clip of me surfing the first part of Flash Flood. No way. All they showed was my tumble over the falls.

It got so bad that I couldn't make a move at school without the cracks ringing out.

"Hey, Willie, you need some help down these stairs?"

"Watch your step, surf chump."

"Have a nice trip?"

By the end of the week, I didn't know what to think. On the one hand, I still wanted to compete in the contest and win. On the other hand, I wished I had never even suggested the idea in the first place.

The fact that Rusty was nowhere to be seen only increased my stress. I closed my eyes and thought of Psalm 37:3–4. Like Rusty said, God would work things out. He knew what was in my heart, and He would do what was best for me.

When I opened my eyes, there he wasn't. No Rusty, which meant no surfboard. When the SurfMaster 1000 floated down in two pieces, Rusty had offered to restore it for me. His years of surfing had also meant years of fixing dings, cracks, broken skags, and on occasion, boards that were snapped in two.

If he had the expertise to restore the SurfMaster, that was fine with me. But today my big concern wasn't the SurfMaster, it was the other board he was going to let me use. Without it, I couldn't even enter the contest.

I searched the back of the parking lot, hoping to see Rusty come cruising up.

Honk! I practically jumped out of my sandals.

Turning around, I saw Rusty in the driver's seat of his van, grinning. Somehow he had snuck up behind me.

"Sorry I'm late," Rusty said through his open window. "I'm afraid I've got bad news. The surfboard I was going to lend you today got messed up on the move out here. The skags were cracked so badly I can't let you use it."

My heart dropped. After everything I had been through, I wouldn't even be able to enter the contest.

"As soon as I saw it, I felt really bad," Rusty went on. He got out and opened the back of the van. "So I decided to do something about it. Today you'll ride my new board."

He reached in and pulled out a brand-new surfboard. It was about seven feet tall and as white as paper. It had red stripes down the sides and cool decals on the deck.

"This is awesome!" I marveled.

"I had it custom-made before I knew I'd be moving. It arrived just before I came here," Rusty said. "No one has ever surfed on it."

I swallowed a few more butterflies. "Maybe I shouldn't be the first."

"Yes, you should. You'll shred on this thing, bro. Oh, and there's one more thing." Rusty directed me to have a look inside the van. The SurfMaster 1000 rested on a bed of carpet, completely restored and looking like new. "I finished it last night and thought I'd bring it along for your victory lap around the Pipeline Lagoon."

"Now *that's* trust," I said. "But I like it."

While Rusty searched for a parking space, I headed for the contest's registration table with the new surfboard under my arm. It felt lighter than one of the butterflies in my stomach. After registering, I stepped inside Tidal Wave, but I didn't get far. I was too stunned to move and stopped for fear I'd trip over my open mouth.

The park looked spectacular, like a tropical paradise transplanted to the outskirts of Glenfield. Every detail was perfect. All kinds of palm trees lined the walkways. Some even featured real coconuts. Alongside, banana, guava, and papaya trees dripped clusters of fruit. Flowers bloomed in planters. Tropical birds called to one another and flew between branches. Streams and waterfalls babbled over rocks and fell into pools. A Beach Boys song played over the loudspeakers.

"Unbelievable," I marveled out loud.

Resuming my walk, I passed by the rides, every one of which was operational. Flash Flood had a long line of kids, each holding inner tubes, ready for the thrill of their lives. Beanstalk spiraled to the clouds, eager riders climbing the leaves. Big Niagara poured one thrill seeker after another over the falls. With the pool filled and deep, they swam to the edge, laughing and raising their arms in victory.

Sky Dive, Splash Fun, and every other ride had long lines of happy kids, raving to each other about the improvements.

When they turned to watch me walk past, it was hard not to wish I was in line with them. Instead, I was on my way to a surf contest as the self-proclaimed winner, even though I had never surfed a wave in my life.

As I neared Pipeline Lagoon, I consoled myself with the hope that maybe everyone had opted for the rides instead of the contest. Other than a few pros, I reasoned, there might not be a soul in sight.

Once again, I was dreaming.

The beach at Pipeline Lagoon was packed. You could barely see the sand because of all the people lounging on blankets and towels. Even the grandstands behind the beach were jammed with spectators. Not only that, Loop-to-Loop had the longest line of all the rides. While kids waited their turn, they stood on the side of Pipeline Lagoon, watching the competitors' area underneath the bleachers.

I found out why as soon I entered. The biggest names in surfing were on hand. Greats like Jeff Mills and Kelly Slater, along with hot newcomers Matt Harber and Ryan Grant, mingled together and talked about surfboards.

The press was also thick, moving from one pro to another, eager for interviews. When I saw Susan Hunter, I wanted to hide, fearful she would come over and make a fool of me in front of everyone. But with all the pros around, she didn't even notice me.

Perfect, I thought. *I'll just fade into the—*

"Plummet!" an angry voice snapped, shoving me from behind.

I stumbled forward and turned around. It was Crusher Grubb. He was holding a six-foot board that looked as new as mine.

"What's up?" I asked.

"Me," Crusher challenged. "I'm up for a win and you're going down."

I swallowed hard and clutched my surfboard like a shield. A few of the pros stepped over to see what was going on.

"Stay off my waves or else," Crusher warned, pushing past me. "By the way, I saw you on the news. Nice ride, goofball." With that he let out a laugh and made his way toward one of the reporters.

"Hey, bro, don't let him get to you," Matt Harber said. "Anyone can talk trash."

Ryan Grant also stepped over. "That's right. It's what happens in the water that counts." He gave me a slap on the shoulder. I shook my head in wonder, surrounded by surfing greats.

Moments later the announcer came over the loudspeaker. "Ladies and gentleman, welcome to

Tidal Wave's first annual Pro-Am Surf Contest."
Everyone cheered in response.

The announcer explained the rules of the contest,
then directed our attention to the long rock overhang
at the back of Pipeline Lagoon. "Join me in welcom-
ing the first wave of the day."

We watched as a swell suddenly emerged from
the back and rolled forward. Halfway to the beach,
the wave's face rose up and peaked in a vertical wall
of water easily eight feet high. Moments later the
wave's lip pitched forward and curled, peeling in both
directions as it rolled to the beach.

At first, the crowd grew silent, in awe of the
wave's perfect shape. But once it reached the beach,
everyone erupted with applause. Even the pros nodded with approval.

"This rules."

"Gnarly."

"Rad."

"Psycho shape."

"Hot."

I felt the same way. What a victory for Felix's dad.
Despite countless obstacles, it all had come together.
This had to do wonders for Felix's trust level. He and
his dad probably were in the rock area right now, cel-
ebrating. They had worked around the clock to get
ready for this day, and they'd made it.

When the announcer came on again, it was to
invite all the contestants into the water for an hour of

practice before the contest began. That was all the
pros needed to hear. Before I took one step, they were
rushing past me for the lagoon. Crusher was in the
thick of them and managed to give me a shove as he
went by.

"Now I'll never catch a wave," I muttered in frustration, "not with Crusher and all those pros in the
water." Then again, maybe that wasn't such a bad
thing. The first waves would be the most closely
watched. After the initial excitement died down, I
could paddle out and catch a few waves before the
warm-up session came to an end.

"Willie, what are you doing here?" a voice asked.

"Not again," I moaned, still uptight about Crusher's threat.

Sam came up behind me. She was wearing a
bathing suit and holding a wireless microphone.

I relaxed and buried my feet in the cool sand.
"Getting ready to find Felix. Why? What are you doing
here? Looking for another chance to embarrass me?"

"Don't make me feel guilty about that again," Sam
pleaded. "I've already apologized to you at least a
hundred times."

"I know. I'm just kidding. So what's your assign-
ment now that you're an official news reporter?" I
asked.

"I began by interviewing the kids taking the
rides," Sam said. "But now that the surfing has started, I'm going to cover the action from the water."

"From the water? How can you talk into a micro-phone when a wave is crashing over your head?"

"I'll stay near the back, where the wave is form-ing," Sam explained. "They have a longboard I can sit on to do interviews. Plus, it's a waterproof micro-phone. So if it gets wet, no big deal."

"Speaking of interviews, you should talk to Felix's dad. He's the brains behind all this."

"That's a good idea. Since you're not paddling out right now, why don't you go find him and set it up," Sam suggested. "I'll interview him after I get done in the water."

"Sounds good," I said.

We walked along the side of the lagoon, past where the waves were breaking. From there Sam made her way into the water to the board that was waiting for her. I kept going to the rock overhang at the deep end of Pipeline Lagoon. After a little search-ing, I found a door in the rocks. It led to a flight of stairs that went down to a large cavern. The cavern was filled with the machinery that produced the waves. There were giant pipes everywhere, along with hydraulic pumps—everything you needed to produce perfect man-made waves. Of course there was one exception—a man. There wasn't a person in sight. *Talk about automation*, I thought. *This baby runs on its own.*

"Felix? Mr. Patterson?" I called out, determined to find them. I made my way to the end of the room.

The air felt damp and heavy from all the water sloshing and waves crashing overhead. Reaching a door, I
opened it up, not at all prepared for what I'd find.

Making Waves

Felix's dad sat on a metal chair, staring at a control board. His elbows were propped on the counter in front of him. Drops of sweat glistened on his face. He looked like the most tired man on earth, ready to pass out.

Felix stood behind him on the tile floor, squeezing his shoulders. "Hang in there, Dad."

"There you are, Mr. Patterson," I said, letting the door close behind me. "I came here to congratulate you."

Still staring at the controls, Felix's dad made an adjustment. It was as if I didn't exist.

"I said, I came to congratulate you, Mr. Patterson. Everything looks fantastic, especially Pipeline Lagoon," I repeated.

Again, no response. Mr. Patterson only took his eyes off the control board to check the video monitors resting on a shelf above him. Each had a different shot of the lagoon.

Realizing that Felix's dad was a little too busy and too tired to acknowledge my presence, I decided to try Felix.

"Aloha, dude," I said, shaking his arm. "How are the waves?"

"Hey!" Felix shot back. "Knock it off."

"What's wrong?" I asked.

Felix moved back from his dad and spoke in a low voice. "Everything. My dad got practically no sleep last night—or all week for that matter. Then, to make things worse, his assistant came down with chicken pox."

"Does that mean you get to operate the wave machine today?" I teased. "Mr. Minnow Toes, himself. *Heh, heh.* Get it?"

"Sure, I get it," Felix said. "You bagged on my lotion and mask. But I'm not sick, am I?"

"That's a good point," I said.

I looked at Mr. Patterson. His head rocked back and forth like it was ready to drop. Felix quickly moved back to the control board. I did the same, ready to hold up his dad's head if needed.

"Why do the controls have to be watched so closely?" I asked, feeling sorry for Mr. Patterson. "Isn't the wave machine automatic?"

"Yes," Felix replied. "But because the machinery is new, adjustments are still needed. The sand bottom also makes things tricky. Other wave pools are cement. The sand is more realistic, but it's also more difficult to work with because it's constantly changing."

The monitors captured one wave after another emerging from the back of the lagoon and rolling toward the beach.

"Looks like you have it down, Mr. Patterson," I said.

He murmured in response, like he was talking in his sleep.

"There's one more thing," Felix went on. "My dad designed the wave machine to produce different kinds of waves. Some have crumbly slopes; others have big hollow barrels. It all comes down to the control panel, which means more pressure on the controller."

"Pressure? It sounds like fun. Let me try." I reached toward the panel, but Felix caught my hand and shoved it away. In the process I knocked his bottle of lotion to the floor.

"Hands off!" Felix shouted. "Do you want to ruin the entire contest?"

"Okay, okay. If you don't want my help, I'm outta here." Or so I thought. I stepped on the lotion bottle and reeled around like I had one foot on a skateboard. "Whoa! Lookout!"

"No!" Felix shouted. He tried to stop me but couldn't.

My body twisted and turned, heading straight for Mr. Patterson. *Crash!*

I sprawled across the control board. Felix's dad was under me, face down. By the time I got to my feet, the monitors were black. The wave machine was silent. And Mr. Patterson was out cold.

"No!" Felix cried in agony. "Dad! Wake up!"

Mr. Patterson didn't respond.

"Dad!" Felix tried again. Still no response.

"Maybe he's just sleeping," I said. "He *really* looked tired."

"He'd be okay if you hadn't bodyslammed his head," Felix shouted. He pulled his dad off the control board and onto the chair. His dad slumped over, still unconscious.

"He's breathing fine," I said, trying to make the best of things.

"I'll call first aid," Felix said. He dialed the number and explained what had happened.

"Well?" I asked.

"They're on the way."

"Awesome. Now what about the wave machine?" I pointed out. "What's wrong with it?"

"Oh, nothing much. Just some guy played dog pile on the control panel," Felix growled. He punched buttons and adjusted every knob he could, but the monitors wouldn't come back on.

"Now what?" I asked.

Felix rummaged through some drawers and found a walkie-talkie and a pair of binoculars. He handed them to me. "Go to the beach and tell me what you see. Describe the wave from the moment it appears until it crumbles on the shore."

"You got it," I said, heading for the door. But before leaving, I stopped. "Felix, don't stress over the surf contest. The main thing is helping your dad. The contest is just for fun. They're only waves."

"Only waves? Willie, there's something I need to tell you. You're standing under the largest wave machine in existence. We have no idea what it's capable of." As Felix finished speaking, a low rumble began to shake the control room.

"What do you mean?" I asked.

"Big waves," Felix said. "*Tidal wave* big."

Sprinting as fast as I could, I rounded the rock area at the back of Pipeline Lagoon, ran along the side of the wave pool, and reached the beach. Staring intently through the binoculars, I watched for the first swell. Soon it appeared from the rock overhang and rolled forward. It was the biggest wave so far, and the pro surfers loved it. Matt Harber made a deep bottom turn, followed by an aerial off the lip. The crowd went wild.

I explained every detail to Felix on the walkie-talkie.

"Now that's a wave," Rusty said, appearing beside me. He held the SurfMaster 1000 under his arm.

"So far so good," I replied. I told him about Felix's dad and the incident in the control room.

We held our breath waiting for the next wave. When it appeared, we nearly gagged. It bulged from the rocks and lumbered for the beach. The crowd grew silent. As a few surfers positioned themselves for the ride, the rest paddled hard to clear the face before it crashed down on their heads. That's when I noticed Sam. She was doing her best to control her microphone and avoid the wave at the same time.

"Paddle harder, Sam!" Rusty yelled. "Forget the mike. Just move!"

I described everything to Felix. The giant wave drew Sam to the peak. It looked like she would drop 20 feet, followed by a ton of water landing on her head. With her free hand, Sam dug deep in the water and paddled. She even hung her feet over the sides and kicked.

It worked. Just as the wave curled, Sam eased down the back side to safety. In front of the wave, Ryan Grant took off late but made the drop and cut hard at the bottom. For a moment the liquid barrel swallowed him, then he shot out of the tube like a bullet, followed by a burst of mist.

The spectators rose to their feet, applauding both the wave rider and wave maker.

"That's big enough, Felix!" I cautioned him. "Maybe too big."

"The controls are messed up," Felix shot back. "I'm having to experiment. Just let me know what happens."

Soon the cheering died down, and we all waited for the next wave. Behind us, it looked like the entire water park had crowded into the bleachers.

It seemed like hours went by as we waited. When the first sound reached us, I knew something was wrong. A loud rumble echoed across the water, like a battalion of tanks.

"Check it out," Rusty gasped.

From the rock overhang at the back of Pipeline Lagoon, a mountain of water began to rise. Unlike the other swells that had just appeared, this one took its time, growing wider and higher by the second.

At first the crowd was too shocked to speak. Then a woman changed all that by screaming at the top of her lungs, "Tidal wave!"

Others on the beach joined in. "Run for your lives!"

"We're doomed."

"Every man for himself."

"Women and children first."

"Mayday! Mayday!" I shouted into the walkie-talkie. "Felix, it's a tidal wave! Shut the machine down! Quick!"

Felix didn't answer. I prayed that he had heard my message, but I couldn't take time to talk anymore. My concern was for Sam. She'd barely cleared the last wave. This one would land on her head like the *real* Niagara Falls. She might not surface for weeks.

Rusty read my mind. "Sam's got to get out of there."

The tidal wave rolled toward her, rising higher and higher. Instead of a peak, it was a massive wall, hungry to flatten anything in its path. Sam tried to paddle to deeper water, to get over the wave before it curled.

But she didn't have a chance.

A Ride to Die For

"Here, I'll trade you," I said to Rusty. I handed him the walkie-talkie and binoculars in exchange for the SurfMaster 1000. Taking it under my arm, I wove through the spectators as they rushed for higher ground.

"Go for it, bro!" Rusty called after me. "You're ready!"

I ran into the Pipeline Lagoon. Water splashed under my feet. I pushed ahead until I was knee deep in the water, then I jumped on the SurfMaster and hit the power button. The jet engine launched me forward. Lying on my stomach, I kept paddling to increase my speed.

The tidal wave was just a few seconds from Sam. It loomed over her like a mountain of water. I thought the wave looked big from the beach, but from my surfboard it looked like I was staring up at Mount Everest.

"Hang on, Sam," I shouted. The wave's face rose to vertical, casting a shadow. Every surfer in the water paddled hard to get away. Some rose over the giant swell; others made it to the side.

But not me. I was stroking straight into its massive jaws to save Sam.

But she didn't even notice me. Sam just kept doing her job. With the waterproof microphone in hand, she chattered away for the spectators. She was determined to report the news, even to the bitter end.

I paddled hard. Twenty more feet and I'd be there. Ten. Five.

"Sam! Get ready to jump!" I yelled at her.

When she turned to look, I could see the fear in her eyes. But she stayed calm. "Folks, say hello to Willie Plummet! Without his initiative, this contest would never have happened," I heard her say.

I paddled on. Only a few more feet.

Sam sat in the bowl of the tidal wave. Its thick lip rose over her, frothing with white foam and ready to drop.

One last stroke. Yes!

"Quick, hop on!" I shouted, turning beside her. Sam hesitated.

"Hurry," I repeated.

Still clutching the microphone, Sam scrambled from her board to the SurfMaster. She kneeled on the midsection, just in front of me.

"Now hang on," I warned her.

As the giant tidal wave curled over our heads, I rose to my feet. Leaning heavily on my back foot, I sliced through the giant tube. It felt like a liquid tunnel large enough to drive a semi through. Talk about a huge barrel. I could've been 10 feet tall and still not gotten my hair wet.

Sam spoke into the microphone, commenting on every sight and sound. It was definitely spectacular, like a liquid green room. Too bad it wouldn't last.

The only daylight visible was 50 feet in front of us at the end of the tube. On a regular surfboard, we never would have made it. But thank God for the Surf-Master 1000. I leaned forward and kicked it into high speed. We lunged ahead, peeling along the wall of the barrel. With the curl arching over us, it felt like we were standing behind a waterfall. If only we could get to the open end before it closed out completely and crushed us like ants.

"Another 20 feet and we'll make it," Sam said into the microphone.

I gritted my teeth, thinking we never would. Then I remembered what God had been teaching me all along. Trust in Him. *I can't do it, God, but You can*, I thought.

I edged the board higher on the wave, then dropped down to pick up speed. As the space in the curl grew smaller, I crouched down.

Ten more feet. Five.

The ceiling of the barrel touched my hair. I squatted as low as I could.

Three more feet. Two.

"Banzai!" I shouted.

The curl closed tightly just as we hit the end. I squeezed the side of the board and lowered my head, unwilling to give up. We hit the curl like a torpedo and kept going into the open air.

"Yes!" I wailed.

"Unbelievable!" Sam announced into the waterproof microphone.

The roar of the crowd joined the sound of crashing water. Sam's broadcast had been played live for the spectators. At the first sight of us, the people in the bleachers went wild.

But our ride wasn't over. The side of Pipeline Lagoon, a solid cement wall, was coming fast. Even if we jumped from the SurfMaster, we'd skip across the water and smash into it.

Then I saw a way out. Loop-to-Loop. It was a long shot, but we could make it.

Turning hard, I cut over what was left of the wave's shoulder. We launched into the air, straight for Loop-to-Loop. Sam hung on for dear life. So did I.

We sailed over the side wall. *Splash*! We landed in the trough of Loop-to-Loop and kept going. Up the chute. Higher and higher into the loop.

"Hang on!" I wailed.

The SurfMaster kept going. Soon we were vertical. Then inverted. *Swoosh!* We made it through the loop and zoomed into the next one.

But our speed began to slow. We'd never make the second loop. I warned Sam to get ready for a giant turn. As soon as we were vertical, I dug in with my heel and whipped the board around. Going with the water flow really increased our speed. We quickly flew back through the first loop and launched into Pipeline Lagoon.

Once we splashed down, I raised my arms in celebration. We watched as the tidal wave's white foam swallowed the beach all the way to the bleachers. There it finally stopped and eased back into the lagoon.

Then the surface grew calm. That was my cue. I steered the SurfMaster to the beach. As soon as we stepped foot on sand, the reporters and crowd rushed forward to greet us.

"How'd you do it?" one reporter asked.

"I trusted God," I said.

Sam was quick to agree. She also gave a quick description of the SurfMaster 1000. With so many people crowded around us, I didn't see Felix until he was right beside me.

"Sorry about the tidal wave," he said quietly. "But the good news is, my dad's going to be okay."

"Sorry?" I laughed. "Everyone, I'd like to introduce Felix Patterson, the Wave Master himself. If it wasn't for his caution in avoiding chicken pox, this day might not have been possible."

Immediately the attention of the reporters turned to Felix. They were all compliments, wanting to know how he had produced the largest man-made wave of all time and if he had plans to open other parks around the world.

Felix's downcast demeanor changed in a hurry. "Before I begin a world tour, I'd like to begin a surf contest right here. So if you'll excuse me, I've got some work to do."

After he returned to the control room, Felix and his dad only needed a half hour to get things going. The contest began, and pros and amateurs alike rode one perfect wave after another.

It took me awhile to get used to Rusty's surfboard, but I finally got the hang of it. I had several good rides and one off-the-lip turn. When the scores were totaled, I finished third in the contest. At first that kind of bummed me out, but I realized that, given my experience and everything I'd been through, third place was a huge blessing. Crusher Grubb finished second, and a kid from out of town finished first.

Jeff Mills won the pro division with ease.

Standing on the winner's platform, I expected Crusher to rub in the fact that he had finished ahead of me. Instead, he just shook my hand and said, "Good job." I think the tidal wave knocked some sense into him and he was just happy to be alive.

Sam was given the job of interviewing all the winners. And from the expression on the director's face, I could tell he was impressed.

So was I, but not just with Sam and Felix. Most of all, I was impressed with God. Sam, Felix, and I all had our own kinds of success in mind, but God had a different and much better plan for us. No, I didn't come in first, but the lesson I learned was worth far more. Through mountains of rock and mountains of water, God taught us to trust Him to work things out according to His perfect plan. With Him anything is possible.

Collect all **20** books in the series

Look for all these **exciting WiLLiE PLUMMET** misadventures at your local Christian **bookstore!**